HER MARINE BODYGUARD

by

HEATHER LONG

 CB

Decadent Publishing Company
www.decadentpublishing.com

Her Marine Bodyguard
Copyright 2015 by Heather Long
ISBN: 978-1-61333-786-8
Cover design by Mina Carter

Published by Decadent Publishing Company
www.decadentpublishing.com

Printed in the United States of America

Letter to the Readers

Dear Readers,

Two years ago, I introduced you to Second Lieutenant Brody Essex and Shannon Fabray. They met during a 1Night Stand in the book *Her Marine* and—I admit it—I fell a little bit in love with Brody. He was a strong guy, determined. While on leave, he stepped in for one of his fellow Marines (or so he thought) and met a woman who took his breath away. By the end of the story, Brody had to return to his duty station and say goodbye to Shannon. I knew from the moment I wrote the scene that I wanted to see these characters again, but that it would take time before Brody could come home.

What you have here is his homecoming. We caught glimpses of Brody and Shannon in other books—Brody's call to Zach and Logan about Jazz during *No Regrets, No Surrender*, later Liam Gardiner's introduction to Shannon in *A Marine and a Gentleman* and Shannon's cameo in *A Candle for a Marine* and once more, Brody was mentioned during *Have Yourself a Marine Christmas*. Not once in the sixteen books that followed *Her Marine* did I forget that Brody and Shannon were waiting—he was waiting to come home and she waited for him to get there.

I always knew what the story would entail when I brought Brody and Shannon back together—and while they'd maintained their relationship long distance, there is a very distinct difference for a couple to come together after so much time apart. This same challenge faces so many of our military servicemen and women and the significant others who love them.

Brody never had anyone waiting for him before and

Shannon lived with the constant worry that something could happen to him. They each had to be strong for the other. Life went on at home, Brody couldn't be there with her to meet challenges she faced and sometimes weeks could go by without word from him. It's damned hard and it takes a lot of determination on both sides for these kinds of couples to withstand the pressure.

When I sat down to write this novel, it was like coming home for me, too. I'd waited so long to write those words, they were burned into my brain and poured out onto the page. I hope you enjoy Shannon and Brody's reunion as much as I did.

Semper fi,
Heather

~Dedication~

For my readers. You Rock.

Prologue

Camp Leatherneck, Afghanistan

Lieutenant Brody Essex threw the baseball up and caught it, only to repeat the motion. For three weeks, he and his team had been stuck in a holding pattern waiting for the final orders to be cut that would send them to Bagram and from there, aboard a C-130 for Camp Lejeune, North Carolina, debriefing, psych evaluations, and finally he would discuss his terminal leave—if approved.

Of course, all of that required he get back to the States. His unit's exodus, like his promotion and so many other day-to-day issues, remained tied up in bureaucracy. Keeping the ball in motion, he concentrated on patience. Each day brought him a step closer to seeing Shannon again.

Maybe he'd even sneak up to Boston and surprise her at her show. She'd been so excited when she'd Skyped a month before—the last time they'd had to chat.

A rapid three-beat knock hit his door. Brody caught the ball and sat up. "Come."

"Lieutenant, there's a call for you in Coms." The private wasn't one Brody recognized.

Rising, he retrieved his cover from the shelf and set the ball in its place. The room—one he split with another lieutenant—remained bare of anything personal. He and his team hadn't planned on staying. The forced inactivity coupled with the transition state had him less inclined to make his mark.

"Dismissed," he told the private and followed him out. Maybe the call included his orders. When he'd last checked, Colonel Jamison had told him his orders would get there when they got there. Until then, stand by. Like Brody, the rest of his unit waited, their patience dust-covered and grim-faced after months of dodging and delivering gunfire, seeing comrades killed, tracking targets across the countryside, and sleeping on dirt more often than a bed.

Marinestan had been an upgrade of sorts. Two sergeants stood having a smoke, and they straightened, saluting him as he passed. He returned the gesture and eyed the butts on the ground. One sergeant shifted, put his boot over them and nodded. They'd police the area before they left it. Noting their names, Brody kept walking.

In the building housing Coms, a private directed him to a black phone with a flickering light indicating a call on hold. The private moved away, a tacit offer of privacy.

Retrieving the handset, Brody hit the button. "Essex."

"Brody, Luke Dexter." The former Marine had been Brody's commanding officer for his first three tours and his friend for longer. Also, the absolute last voice he expected to hear.

Spine stiffening and his blood running cold, he frowned but kept his voice low and controlled. "Sir? What's wrong?" Because Luke had no reason in the world to pull strings and get a call put through to Afghanistan. None except....

"It's Shannon. She was attacked...."

Chapter One

"*I* told you that you were going to be a hit." Liam Gardiner put a hand to the open elevator doors, holding them and allowing Shannon Fabray to precede him.

She glanced at her host and laughed. "Yes, you did, and thank you for saying I told you so."

After sliding his hands into the pockets of his slacks, he walked with her toward her room. He'd initially invited her to stay at his townhouse, but she'd declined. Most men made her uncomfortable, and though she'd gotten to know Liam better over the last several months and knew without a shred of doubt he was no threat to her physically or romantically, she'd preferred the privacy of the hotel. It made her more comfortable.

Like her, Liam waited for his Marine to come home. "How is Brenden?" she asked.

"He's good. Always has a new story when he calls. I didn't realize how *interesting* Embassy duty could be." A hint of a smile softened his mouth. Vice-president of a local bank, he possessed a quiet, determined charm and impeccable taste. He'd been passionate about advocating her show, helping her with the venue negotiations, facilitating arrangements from the backers to the show itself, and finally escorting her tonight.

"And how long 'til Brody is home?"

They had a pact, the two of them, for mutual support and general bitching as needed—Liam's words, not hers.

"Soon, I think." Excitement bubbled in her stomach. "He's due to be back in North Carolina anytime now, I just don't know exactly when. Apparently, dates are flexible when it comes to PCSing from combat to relief—or however that goes." She still didn't get all of the military terminology, despite all her lessons over the last two years.

Two years. It made her head spin. Two years since she'd met Brody and more than a year since she'd gone to Italy and met him for a long, fabulous week. Both seemed like a lifetime before.

At her room, Liam gave her a quizzical look. "Are you all right?"

"I'm fine," she covered and dug her room key out of her purse. "Tired." Worried about everything. "Thank you for tonight, really—it meant the world to me."

"You're very welcome, just wait and see, you're going to be a huge hit. I bet you'll be swimming in orders by tomorrow."

Laughing at his optimism, she inserted the room key and waited for the lock to flash from red to green before she pushed the door open. One moment she leaned her weight on the door, half-turned to bid Liam a good night, and the next, she fell as the door yanked wide open. Stars burst when her head collided with the wall by the door. A foot caught her in the shoulder, and she bit off a scream at the fresh bruise of pain.

Liam shouted, and she struggled to sit up, wincing as the door slammed into her shoulder. Across the hall, he grappled with a man and then crashed into the wall. Masculine grunts filled the air, along with the sound of fists striking a body. Fumbling with her purse, she got out the mace, but too late—

the man in black thrust away from Liam and raced down the hall.

"Shannon?" Climbing to his feet, Liam glanced in the direction the assailant fled and then hurried over to her. Blood trickled from the corner of his mouth, and he braced the door to get it off of her. "Hey? You okay?"

Voices came from the other end of the hall. "Are you all right?"

"I called security."

Raising a hand to her head, Shannon found a tender spot. She winced and let Liam pull her to her feet. Blood spotted her fingertips. More guests filled the hallway. Apparently, the commotion had garnered some attention.

The expression on Liam's face became taut, and his mouth compressed. He looked past her, and she turned to find the whole room in shambles. Drawers from the dresser were open and emptied, her clothes scattered everywhere. Her art case tipped on its side on the bed and her sketchbooks lay haphazardly.

Her pulse jackhammering, she stepped toward the destruction. He wrapped an arm around her shoulders and halted her.

"Wait," he said and rounded toward a fresh wave of voices. "Security is coming, let's let them go in first."

But Shannon pulled away, stepping farther into the room despite the flood of panic. Where was it? Where was her—

And then she saw the gleam of silver. Her laptop sat on the floor. It had fallen off the bed. She didn't use it for much, but she kept all her records on it.

Moments later, security entered and had questions, too.

It had already been late when she and Liam left the gallery opening and he'd driven her back to the hotel. Later still after the Boston police took her statement and a paramedic attended the bump on her head. Despite both the paramedic's recommendation and Liam's advice, she decided against going to the hospital. The police needed her to inventory the room and determine if anything had gone missing.

Nothing was.

The hotel offered her a different room on a higher floor, with more amenities. Liam wanted her to come back to his townhouse. She elected to move hotels entirely, taking one closer to the airport since she was scheduled to fly back to Dallas the next day. To play it safe, Liam suggested registering under an alias, and she was too tired to disagree.

"I don't think that's a good idea." Liam passed his credit card to the bartender after he brought her a glass of white wine. He had a beer, a split lip, and what promised to be a black eye.

"It's one glass, and it will settle my nerves." She didn't mention her headache or the gut-wrenching churning going on in her stomach.

"Let me buy you something to eat to go with it." He didn't wait for her response before he gestured to the bartender. "Sandwiches—Reubens and fries."

Shannon took a sip of the wine and concentrated on keeping her hands steady. Anxiety attacks were not new to her. "I'm not sure that I'm hungry, Liam. And your eye looks terrible."

The banker gave her a crooked grin and then held out his phone. "Do me a favor and take a picture."

Setting the wine glass on the bar, she aimed the phone at him and couldn't disguise her shaking. "Why am I taking a picture?"

"Brenden," he said, eyeing the camera steadily until she managed to snap two photos in quick succession. "A black eye is pretty badass."

"Badass?" Though she appreciated his friendship, she didn't always understand him.

"Badass," he reaffirmed with a wry smile. He slipped the phone back into his pocket and held up his right hand. "Skinned knuckles. I did some damage of my own. Black eye says I took a punch. Bruised knuckles said I gave as good as I got. I just wish I hadn't let the bastard get away."

"It's all right." She meant that, too. "You read about people breaking into hotels all the time. I just didn't expect it to happen to me." Reclaiming her wine glass, she took another sip. The bartender returned with the hot sandwiches and fries.

At least she'd changed out of the evening dress. In jeans and the dark gray Marine sweatshirt, she felt safer, shielded. The change of hotels, even the pseudonym, added to her feeling of security. She and Liam said nothing, tucking into their sandwiches, and she was hungrier than she realized.

The food, coupled with the wine, settled her further. "I think I owe you another thank you."

"For?" He sat sideways after having demolished his sandwich and most of his fries.

"For insisting on escorting me back." She hadn't forgotten the fact she'd argued with Liam's offer initially, not seeing the sense of him paying a valet charge just to take her upstairs.

"Don't forget my swift defense. Though it would have been better if he hadn't tried to trample you in the process." With a wink, Liam gave her another crooked grin, which highlighted his split lip. "But you're welcome and when you're ready, I'll walk you to your room here, too. What time is your flight tomorrow?"

"Evening, after six. I thought I'd do some sightseeing, but since it's nearly two in the morning, I think I'll sleep and try to reorganize my sketchbook." After her sketchbook, the most valuable thing in the room had been her laptop. She'd not brought much in the way of jewelry. What few pieces of worth she owned, she'd worn for the gallery opening. "He tore a couple of pages." But she had all the pieces—she could put them back together.

"Sketches can be replaced. How's your head?"

"It aches." Grimacing, she touched a hand to the tender spot on her scalp. She hadn't needed stitches, fortunately. Her shoulder twinged, too, but she kept that information to herself.

"I'm going to get the room right next to yours and stay here at the hotel tonight."

The offer startled her. "You don't have...."

"No, I don't." Liam agreed. "I'll do it anyway. I've had a beer and shouldn't drive, and if you change your mind and want to do some sightseeing—well, I'll be here." He motioned to the bartender then gestured at her near-empty glass. "Want another glass of wine?"

The cramping in her stomach relaxed. She blinked back an unsettling urge to cry and shook her head. "One is enough for me. But I wouldn't mind sitting here a little longer."

"Then we'll sit here." He fished out his phone and set it on the bar. "Better to remind myself nothing is private. The whole world is connected. While drinking, that stays where I can see it."

She must have looked quizzical because he laughed.

"Nothing is sacred. Anyone can overhear. Anyone can video you and plaster it on YouTube or social media." He shrugged. "Seeing my 'smart' phone helps me make smarter choices."

"You're a very complicated guy." Still, she found the presence of the phone oddly comforting. A reminder of the real world and it helped to puncture the surreal bubble surrounding her since they'd had the bad luck to interrupt someone trying to rob her hotel room.

The bartender returned with Liam's fresh beer. When Liam held it up, she raised her wine glass. "What are we toasting?"

"New beginnings. I guarantee you the gallery showing tonight is not going to be your last."

Shannon hesitated before taking another sip. "Kind of feels like jinxing myself."

"Then I'll drink to it, and when it all happens, I can say I told you so." The smug tease in his tone amused her. "Watch me. I told you so about this, and it only took me six months to convince you to say yes to this show."

Her face warmed, because he wasn't wrong. Maybe because of the circumstances of the evening, maybe because they'd actually become friends over the last few months—or maybe she simply missed Brody. Their last Skype call had been limited, and Brody had warned her he could be in and out of touch until he returned to the States.

"Shannon?"

Blinking, she smiled apologetically. "Sorry, I was thinking...anyway...yes, you did tell me it would be successful."

"But?" he prompted, eyebrows raised.

"But, I'm not cut out for this type of thing."

"What type of thing?" Liam frowned.

"Traveling, appearing...talking about my work." God, she wished she'd already flown home and sat in her studio rather than in this hotel. Draining her wine, she put the glass on the bar. She wished Brody were home more—and even that left her stomach knotting. What if his coming home didn't turn out the way she hoped? *The way we hope. Does he share the same hopes?*

A hand came to rest atop hers and squeezed gently. "You're over-thinking all of this. It's late, you're tired, and it's been stressful day. You don't have to think you're going to be fabulous. I can do all of that for you."

Another laugh broke free, and it sounded an awful lot like a sob, so she swallowed the sound and tugged away from his grasp. Bracing her palm over her mouth, she tried to stifle her seesawing emotions.

"I'm sorry," she whispered.

"No apologies required." Always a gentleman, Liam pulled a handkerchief out of his pocket. "Remember, I know fabulous when I see it."

Accepting the pressed linen, she dabbed at her eyes and gazed at him with curiosity. "Do I dare ask why?"

"Of course you can ask why." His crooked grin deepened, but so did the kindness in his eyes. "I'm fabulous. Just ask anyone—even better, ask Brenden. He's known my fabulousness for years."

This time when Shannon laughed, the emotion felt real.

Dallas, Texas
Two days later....

Fortunately, the rest of her visit went pleasantly. Liam managed to lure her back out of the hotel for a few hours to return to the gallery. He'd made a game of it and they'd gone *incognito* so Shannon could see how visitors were enjoying her work. With a hat to hide her hair and at Liam's snarky assistance, she found watching others while they viewed her work far more comfortable than she'd imagined.

Her agent called three times, each with a higher offer for *Her Marine*, the centerpiece of her gallery exhibit. No matter how often she'd told Henry she had no interest in selling the work, he continued to call her with the latest offers. He described it as motivational, and since the most recent one had climbed to six figures, he'd started to lean in favor of the buyers.

She relaxed while the cab weaved through heavy evening traffic. Temperatures were expected to be in the 90s. Unlike most of the nation, Texas hadn't suffered through a brutal winter, and spring had segued to summer without pausing to take a breath.

The closer to her converted loft she got, the better she felt. Traveling wasn't easy for her—another symptom of old fears better to be forgotten. She'd made huge strides in the last two years. Brody never gave her a grief about the panic attacks, though those had grown fewer and further between. All she had to do was think about him when things grew tough and the tension winding through her would ease.

At least the headache the bump on the head had earned her hadn't followed her home. A couple of ibuprofen and a Xanax before her flight and she'd been back to normal. The cab slowed, turned the last corner for her place, and eagerness threaded through her veins.

Home.

She wanted to repair the damage to her sketches, review the ideas she had under consideration, and then get to work. If she immersed herself in a project, she could stop wondering when she'd hear from Brody. *He's okay. Not hearing doesn't mean bad news.* They'd gone as long as twelve weeks between contacts, but Brody warned her whenever those lags might occur.

The driver parked in front of her building. "Ma'am?"

"Oh, sorry." She glanced at the total and counted out the bills, adding a generous tip. After passing the cash to him, she waited while he wrote a receipt. At least she'd remembered to get receipts on this trip. Her agent and her accountant had both reminded her regularly to keep track of her expenses.

Five minutes later, she had the main door unlocked and set her case inside. The best part of her loft was the private entrance and steel security door. Her mail had accumulated inside, so she left the suitcase and scooped all of the envelopes up to carry with her. The main floor sat empty, waiting to be converted into a gallery later. She had a basket elevator to access the upstairs where she lived and housed her studio. The main room of her place included one large work area with plastic sheeting draping half the tables while the others featured smaller practice pieces.

Dumping the mail on the kitchen table, she passed by her work area to say hi to all her guys. Though *Her Marine* remained her most popular work, she'd shied away from doing other military pieces—at least publicly. Six pieces sat on the workbench, and she studied each one...they were all men she'd met thanks to Brody.

A lean, broad-shouldered Marine stood with his arms folded and a remote expression on his face. The face had proved the hardest to capture, scarring had left its mark on his left cheek. It was close, but in miniature, very difficult to detail the nuances. And while Logan scared the hell out of her, he hadn't been remotely unkind.

Bypassing that work, she went to the next one. The young man stood solemnly, staring down at the dog next to his feet. Squatting, Shannon considered the pair. It had taken her three attempts to get the dog correct and she still didn't think she'd done Jethro any favors. She's wanted to capture the beautiful Labrador with his soulful eyes and the sense of his playfulness.

The next two statues were more straightforward. Zach Evans had beautiful bone structure—and frankly too pretty to ever be a Marine. But what did she know? The photograph she'd worked from featured him smiling at his wife. His smile, like Logan's before him, still didn't seem quite right. She hadn't quite mastered the tenderness in it.

Damon was the fourth statue, and she'd done him up in the chef hat and all. She'd used photos from the Mike's Place brochure and their advertising materials. Rebecca Dexter had even sent her a couple of larger photos when Shannon asked about them. Fortunately, Rebecca hadn't asked why she'd needed them, except to say when she had the room in her schedule, Rebecca wanted a commission of Luke.

The piece sat waiting for her—unfinished as it was. Rebecca had provided a photo of a younger Luke in his full dress blues and another of him on his wedding day. She wanted something like the composition of *Her Marine*, only without the nudity. The difference in the figures, posed back to back, struck her immediately. The rigidity of the man in uniform and his taciturn expression suggested he was every bit the weapon, but the man in the suit showed a gentler side; careworn, and aged...but no one could mistake the laughter.

That piece was the best so far, but would take the longest to finalize as a life-sized sculpture. The sixth and final one had been the last one she'd completed before having to halt everything to get ready for Boston. A special request, the nude figure wore prosthetics from the knee down on both legs. It would face another mirror, as she'd done with *Her Marine*, only in this one, he would be in his uniform.

The Marine in question, Ryan "Rebel" Brun, had saved Brody's life. She'd met him on a handful of occasions, at Brody's request, and she'd never forgotten the man's spirit and determination. Brody thought the world of Rebel, and he'd told her about the incident in a very quiet, calm voice.

She'd had nightmares for weeks after, nightmares she'd kept to herself. If Brody could be strong telling her, and Rebel so strong in his recovery, what excuse did she have? Even sculpting the work piece had brought the nightmares back.

This one.... It had to be this one she worked on next. She wanted to chase away the bad dreams before he came home. Decided, she left the worktable and headed for her bedroom. Stripping off her travel clothes, she'd barely pulled on one of her favorite work T-shirts when the landline rang. Only a few people had the studio number. Probably Liam making sure she'd arrived home all right. She'd texted him when the plane landed at DFW, but he turned out to be such a mother hen.

"Hello?" When there was no immediate reply, save for the sound of an open connection, she tried again. "Hello?"

Nothing.

Sometimes calls didn't connect all the way through. "Hello? If you're there, and you can hear me, I can't hear you." It had happened a few times over the last couple of months. "Okay, I'm going to hang up. Call me back." Returning the handset to the cradle, she twisted the caller ID box around. She had a cordless phone in the other room—this was an old-style hardwire phone. It would work even in a power outage, but that meant she'd had to add a separate device to track incoming numbers.

It read *caller unknown*.

Damn it. What if it had been Brody? Perching on the edge of her bed, she ran her fingers through her hair and gathered it all back into a ponytail, all the while staring at the phone and practically willing it to ring again.

With regret, she abandoned her post after five minutes. He

would call her back as soon as he could. Getting a bottle of water and the cordless phone, she ignored the mail and went to get her supplies together. Forget the world for a while and focus on the sculpting.

Her work—her art remained the best medicine for her.

Chapter Two

The front door buzzer rang for the third time, and Shannon glared at the intercom. After shutting off the water and setting her chisel aside, she padded across the soaking wet plastic wrap and ignored the spatter dribbling down her legs. She'd thrown open four windows to try and catch a breeze, but she'd have to give in and flip the air conditioning on. Wiping her hands on a towel, she hit the button with her elbow. "Yes?"

"Okay, Rapunzel, send down the elevator. I've got lunch and orders."

Once upon a time, Shannon had envied Lauren Kincaid's husky voice. The actress had made a name for herself on several television shows before conquering the romantic comedy landscape. These days though, she focused her efforts working on local, independent films and living with her fiancé in Allen.

"One sec," Shannon said, because Lauren wouldn't take no for an answer. Through Brody, Shannon had met several of the residents and employees of Mike's Place. The veteran's rehabilitation center served as a halfway point for a number of Marines, soldiers, airmen and more returning home. Lauren's fiancé was the head psychologist and an incredibly kind man.

He also had the most annoying habit of getting Shannon to talk. Lauren had decided they were friends almost from the first, and to be fair, Shannon liked her, too. Shutting off the intercom, she hit the release button that would send the elevator to the ground floor and then hurried over to cover up the works in progress. After working for three days straight, she had just begun to refine the facial features on the first half of the Rebel statue.

After she covered the practice pieces, she didn't have time to run a brush through her hair. The gate slid back to reveal Lauren, promised bags of food in hand. Dressed in beautiful white slacks and a pale, peach tank top, it appeared like she'd stepped off the cover of a fashion magazine. Even her hair fell in perfect waves too obedient to let a stray strand muss her perfect coif.

Shannon wore a ripped T-shirt over a pair of denim cut-off shorts. Her arms and legs were a grayish color, covered in the spatter of her work, and her fingers were scraped raw in several places. They'd hurt like hell when she washed them. Having pulled all of her hair up into a doubled-over ponytail, she imagined it resembled a rat's nest rather than something attractive.

Keys in one hand and bags of takeout Chinese in the other, Lauren paused to press a quick kiss to Shannon's cheek even as Shannon kept her arms wide to avoid dirtying her friend's lovely clothes. "I knew you were working," Lauren said by way of greeting. "Come, sit and eat with me, and then I will get out of your hair."

Left with no choice, Shannon followed her friend to the kitchen. It looked like a disaster area there, too. Her unread mail sat in a stack on the counter, dirty dishes filled the sink, and her coffee pot was the only thing she'd cleaned—and then only to brew fresh three times a day.

Hurrying around Lauren, she went to work stacking the dirty dishes into the dishwasher. Unsurprisingly, Lauren set her items on one clear spot of counter and came over to help her. "I'll do this, you wash your hands and eat."

"You act like I'm not eating when you don't come to visit."

Since it didn't veer far from the truth, Shannon tried to keep the words light.

"I don't doubt that you do, but we all promised to check in on you, and when you get tied up in a new piece, you sort of shut the rest of the world out."

"True." She could admit her own failings. Switching sides with Lauren, she scrubbed her hands under warm water and hissed as the soap stung. Her friend hadn't been there ten minutes, and Shannon already suffered the twinging muscles in her shoulder and along her back—cramped from the way she'd stood and worked her chisel in short, controlled motions.

"Go take a shower, sweetie." Lauren gave her a sympathetic pat. "I'll wash this up and clear a spot for us to eat."

Glancing around the disarray in the living area—her studio had overtaken virtually all of it—Shannon sighed with embarrassment. Obsessed with the new work, she'd let the days melt together, but apparently work had let the mess melt together, too.

"Seriously, go," Lauren told her while making shooing motions. "You forget, I know what it's like to immerse myself in a project. Go shower, change your clothes and then we can eat and gossip."

Regret mingled with gratitude and Shannon smiled. "Thank you."

"You're welcome. Now. Move it, missy." Lauren might have a multimillion-dollar face and the sultry girl-next-door perfected to an art form, but she worked well as a drill sergeant, too. Hurrying off to do as she asked, Shannon stripped as soon as she slipped behind the silkscreen divider separating her sleeping area from the studio.

Fifteen minutes later, freshly showered and dressed in clean clothes, she felt enormously better. Lauren had loaded the dishwasher, cleaned off the counters, and had begun sorting the mail into different stacks.

"Okay, now you're really going too far." The mail stack was ridiculous. She'd been so busy before going to Boston, and then away, that the number of envelopes had reached precarious heights.

"I'm mostly getting all the junk mail off to one side, and I can take it and drop it in the recycle bin on my way out. Identifiable bills here, anything art-related here, and junk here." She tapped each stack. "Eat and tell me about Boston."

Who'd told her? Liam had no reason to call anyone about the break in at the hotel. Yes, she had a bump on the head, but frankly he'd gotten the worse end of it with his black eye. Lauren nudged one of the containers over. "It's moo goo gai pan, your favorite. And the show, silly. How did the gallery opening go?"

"Oh." Shannon rubbed a hand over her face. "Maybe I'm more tired than I thought." But her friend gave her an odd look. Determined to blow past her own silliness, Shannon opened the carton and chopsticks. At least this she needed no help with. The noodles and the chicken were perfect, so were the mushrooms. In between bites, she said, "The show opened really well, I think. Jeanine and Henry were thrilled about the reviews and a lot of the pieces had bids or sold during the event."

Jeanine had called the night before, long enough to tell her Henry continued to fend off their very insistent buyer, but he'd increased the offer to half-a-million. The amount was ridiculously high, but *Her Marine* meant more to her than money, and she refused to sell.

"That's so awesome," Lauren said, and frowned at one of the thicker envelopes in the stack.

"Stop being my secretary and come talk." She felt guilty about Lauren doing so much of the work.

"I am. It's just...I've had letters like this. How often are you getting these?" The padded manila envelope seemed as innocuous as others in the stack.

Shrugging once, Shannon continued to devour her lunch.

Her stomach seemed to practically weep in relief. Apparently, she'd foregone one too many meals. "I have no idea, I'm about six weeks behind really reading any of my mail." All of her bills were paid via autopay, or she'd be left to work in the dark. "Most of the business stuff goes to Jeanine and Henry. They deal with it and pass on what I need to look at."

Brody didn't write real paper letters. She did, and she'd sent them to him often in the beginning, holding off only when his unit traveled to new assignments. Iraq. Afghanistan. North Africa. His assignments took him all over the map. But when he stayed in one location long enough, she sent him snail mail. Though he teased her about it and insisted email was fine, she knew he enjoyed the letters.

Email lacked a scent or a texture, or a way to know that what he held in his hand had been in hers. Maybe she romanticized it, but whenever the subject came up on Skype, he couldn't disguise the softness in his eyes. The last two years hadn't been kind to him. She'd seen a hard man harden further, the burdens weighing on him, and if she could give him even the hint of softness, then she'd do it.

"Earth to Shannon," Lauren said, amusement in her smile. "Where did you go?"

Blushing, she didn't mind admitting it to Lauren. "Thinking about Brody."

"That's what I thought. Okay, well, come back to Dallas for a moment." Sobriety stamped out the amusement in her tone. She held up the manila envelope again. "How many of these have you gotten?"

Peering at the envelope, Shannon set her food on the counter and wiped her fingers before reaching to take it. "What is it?"

Instead of passing it over, Lauren held it out of reach. "No, I think we should call James and maybe Luke. Or the cops. Do you know anyone at the Dallas Police Department? I think James knows a couple of them. Damon, too, for that matter."

Her normally sensible friend didn't make any sense. "It's

mail. What do you think it is?"

"Fan mail." The actress set the envelope down carefully. In fact, she'd held it carefully—using only her thumb and forefinger on one corner.

Okay, that was odd. No one sent her fan mail, or maybe they did. But not at her studio...no one but friends came to her studio. Even potential gallery showings were handled by digital presentation, or she went to them. "I don't think it's fan mail. No one would have this address."

Despite being on the phone, Lauren waved her off and held up a finger "Hi, hon, I'm at Shannon's and need a favor. Can you call one of your friends at the DPD? Shannon's got some suspicious mail.... Yes, I used to get envelopes like this before my agent shifted how I got my mail. Then it went through their office."

"Lauren...." Shannon said, but the blonde woman shook her head.

"Yeah, I count at least three here, and we should talk to a cop and maybe someone else about her security."

Sliding around Lauren, Shannon held her hands out wide so the actress didn't think she planned touching the envelope and finally got a look at the front of it.

Mine Artiste

"No," Lauren said. "It doesn't have her address on it. I stopped going through the mail when I found it." She paused, clearly listening to her fiancé. Her sober expression darkened. "Okay, I'm going to wait here with her....yes, I have a taser in my purse along with mace, and I'm not afraid to use them."

Stomach bottoming out, Shannon crossed her arms and backed up to lean against the counter. Once Lauren had drawn her attention to it, she could see at least two similar envelopes in her mail stack. No address. No stamp. Obviously hand-delivered. But by whom? And why?

"James is calling Luke and Damon. Damon's downtown today with Helena, so he'll likely get here first."

"Maybe we're making a big deal out of this?" They could be

something her agent or his wife dropped off. Though, chances were highly unlikely. They'd have simply written "Shannon."

Lauren wrapped an arm around her. "Rule number one: assume the worst. That way we can be pleasantly surprised." With a little pressure, she guided Shannon away from the mail and back to her lunch. But no matter how cool and relaxed Lauren seemed, she still pulled a taser out of her purse.

"Do you think we're going to need that?" But she knew the answer before Lauren said it. "Assume the worst."

"Exactly," she said with a smile. "So, while we're waiting, tell me all about Boston, and don't leave out a single detail."

More nauseous than anything, Shannon shuddered. The random hotel break-in. What if it hadn't been random? Her pulse began to race, and black spots edged her vision. It took force of will to take a breath. "Maybe I should wait."

Worry tightened Lauren's brows, and she frowned. "Why?"

An hour later, Shannon wanted to be anywhere but her studio, surrounded by uniformed police officers, one DPD detective, and four Marines. God, she swam in testosterone. Lauren sat right next to her, a bulwark of feminine support, and Damon Sinclair had planted himself on her right side.

He'd been the first to show up. Fortunately, she knew him well enough not to retreat at the first sight of his fierce expression. Normally genial, he'd inspected every lock in her place and then started making a list of "changes" he wanted her to consider—including a video camera on her front door. His effortless charm left her uncomfortable even if he meant nothing by it. The cops arrived fifteen minutes after Damon, with two more Marines hot on their heels. Logan Cavanaugh and Zach Evans were flip sides of the same coin—it never failed to amaze her how close the two were, because they were so opposite.

Logan seemed ferocious, and the scars on the left side of his face leant a darker air to him, whereas Zach was pure golden beauty to his partner's beast. The two were best friends and married to the same woman. If Damon's charm made her uncomfortable, she didn't know how to cope with Logan and Zach in her space. They seemed to fill the large space. They'd also taken a position between she and the police.

They introduced the fourth Marine as Archer Morgan—he hadn't come with the ones she knew, instead arriving with the Detective Eric Foster. Foster examined the envelopes then sent the two uniformed officers out to ask some questions of her neighbors—not that she had many. The reclaimed warehouse area had grown in popularity with artists like herself.

"Miss Fabray, do I have your permission to open these?" Detective Foster's question was the first one he'd asked her directly. He'd spoken to the officers, to Lauren, and even to Logan and Zach, but not her.

"Yes, that's fine." No quiver betrayed her rapidly escalating heart rate or nerves.

He'd taken a moment to put gloves on before he slit the envelope open. "The most recent one arrived today?"

"I don't know."

"I'm sorry?" His narrowed eyes pinned her, and she suddenly wanted to be anywhere but here.

Lauren wrapped an arm around her shoulders. "Shannon's been traveling and pretty caught up in her work, so she didn't go through her mail. Before lunch, I carried up a bundle with me from the front. The envelope you have there was in that bundle."

Grateful for Lauren's intervention, Shannon tried to rein in her scattering thoughts. "I got home from Boston three—no four days ago. I brought mail up then and I haven't been back down."

"You haven't checked your mail in four days?" The harsh line of his mouth twisted and added to the skepticism layering the question.

"I was working," she said in a low voice. Maybe he didn't understand what she did, but she could get lost in projects for days.

He slid a paper out of the envelope and studied it. Logan and Zach shifted toward him, but photos came out next. "You were in Boston for a gallery opening?" Nothing in his tone betrayed what the contents were.

"Yes." She cleared her throat, and Lauren gave her a gentle squeeze. "It was a huge one. I've never been featured in another city, and I had fourteen pieces—well, fifteen if you count *Her Marine*."

"And how long were you in Boston?" The detective had pulled out his phone and snapped images of the paper and then each of the photos. After returning them to the envelope, he opened the next.

"Two weeks. I had meetings and then worked in the gallery, helping with the arrangement of the pieces. Then they had arranged a private fundraiser dinner." She tried to relax her shoulders, but her neck ached with the tension bunching the muscles. The dinner had proved a grueling affair, but Liam hadn't left her side. He'd been such a wonderful friend to keep everyone at bay and redirecting conversations when her anxiety surged.

"And the opening?" He didn't look at her but at what appeared to be news clippings.

"That was Wednesday evening—last Wednesday."

"How did it go?"

What did any of this have to do with the mail? Could she really have earned some crazy fan in a week?

"Fine."

"You have a half-million dollar offer on one of your pieces and the others went in the low six-figure range. I think it went more than fine."

How the hell did the detective know?

"Leave her alone, Foster." Logan jerked his chin toward the news clippings. "Those are Boston papers."

They were?

The Detective didn't appear moved by Logan's order. "She

29

can answer my questions here or down at the station. Have you ever had any sales in this range before?"

"I haven't done anything wrong."

"No, you haven't." Damon had his phone out. "FYI, my wife is on the line. She'll be listening to the questioning."

Damon's wife, Helena, was an attorney.

Foster turned, the third envelope in hand. "I'm not blaming the victim, boys. Relax. Miss Fabray, you've been in the...sculpting business for a while. But this was your first full gallery show." He held up a news clipping. Shannon recognized the headline from the arts and leisure section of the Boston paper. It declared her debut a smash success. "How active in the art community were you prior?"

"I don't know. Some of my earlier works were featured in shows, but only as one of many. I had a few other pieces commissioned." Critics panned most of her early work as too cold and lacking in passion. "I did some replicas for a few art openings, and other clients." Though never her favorite type of work, she'd needed to pay the bills.

"So to the best of your knowledge, you weren't a celebrity sculptor or anything like that?" Whatever the third envelope contained had his attention, and Logan edged closer, his frown deepening.

"No." She rubbed a hand over her face. She'd thought Lauren overreacted earlier, but the others were so serious she couldn't help the trepidation racing through her system. "I'm not even very active in the art community." Not online or in person. Large groups of people still made her uncomfortable. Stomach clenching, she blew out a breath. "Someone did break into my hotel room in Boston."

Everyone looked at her and she spread her hands. "Nothing was taken. We interrupted them, I think, before they could find anything of value—and I didn't have anything really for them to take except the laptop."

"Who is *we*?" Foster focused on her, and she did her damndest not to fidget under his hard-eyed, assessing gaze.

"Liam Gardiner, he's a friend of mine. He walked me back to my room, but when I went to go in, a man burst out of it." She left off her bump on the head. It wasn't related to the envelopes. In truth, she didn't want it to be related. "We called the hotel security and the police."

"Do you know the name of the officer in Boston?" Foster added a note on his phone and then took more photos of the third envelope and its contents. Odd how he didn't show her what any of it was.

Was that good or bad?

"I have his card." She stood and then hesitated. The officer had given her his card, and she'd put it...where?

"Hang on," Damon said into his phone. "Helena is reaching out to Liam right now and getting the information."

Relieved that part was over, Shannon glanced at the men in her loft, then back at the envelopes. "This isn't that big a deal, is it?"

Instead of answering her question, Foster asked, "Anything else odd happen in the last few weeks?"

"Odd? No. I sculpt. I work a lot in here." She motioned to her loft. "I get a lot of junk mail, and I keep the flyers and the advertisements because I can use them." Sometimes she ran out of drop cloths or needed to cover a surface for a piece to dry on. She had so much debris in the work area she'd made a pact with herself to clean it out at least once a month. Of course, the last time she'd actually cleaned was six months before. It was such a wreck at the moment.

"Boyfriends? Dates? Other social engagements?"

"What?" No. She frowned. "I don't have a boyfriend."

Zach twisted to stare at her and Damon gave her a sidelong look.

"Well, I don't think of Brody as a boyfriend." She backed away from the masculine questioning and sought help with Lauren.

"But you're seeing Brody. You two have been together for a couple of years now." Lauren answered for her then added for the cop's benefit, "Lieutenant Brody Essex, he's deployed at the moment."

Yes, if one could call two weeks in two years together as seeing each other. She adored Brody and missed him, and she couldn't wait for him to come home, but were they really seeing each other? Or was she simply clinging to the lifeline he'd thrown her?

Oh, she needed all of these people out of her place. Pacing away from them, she retreated to one of the windows overlooking the city. From here, she could see the abbreviated skyline of Dallas. The sidewalks below didn't quite teem with people, but it was after lunch and before happy hour.

Quiet time.

The perfect time to get some work done.

Or it would be if all these people weren't here.

"Shannon." Lauren came to stand next to her, and she spoke in a low tone, "I know you don't like this and you want it to be nothing. Maybe it is nothing, but those letters were hand-delivered."

She knew that.

"And I think whatever is in them is making the detective nervous."

"Not nervous, Ms. Kincaid. But I am concerned, particularly because they were hand-delivered. It suggests whoever is sending them knows where you live, Miss Fabray."

Yes, she'd already come to the same conclusion, but hearing the detective say it aloud added to the harsh reality. Chills chased across her skin, and she folded her arms tighter. "Are they threats?"

"Not precisely," Foster said. "I'm not a profiler, but I have been a cop for a long time, and while I don't want to scare you, you need to take this seriously. Can you stand taking a look at the contents? I want to ask you some questions about them."

She angled away, her courage shredding before it could even form. What she wanted to do included throwing up, pushing everyone out, locking the door, and pretending none of this had happened. She could crank the music, turn the water on, and go back to chiseling. Losing herself in the stone would be so much more preferable.

Asking them or telling them? Brody's voice whispered through her memory, and she sucked in a deep breath. The information couldn't hurt her. Running away and sticking her head in the sand could. *God, I wish he was here....*

Squaring her shoulders, she returned toward the kitchen and the counter where Foster stood. Lauren followed her, and Shannon was grateful for her presence.

"Don't touch anything, I'm going to have our lab see if they can lift prints." Foster laid the contents out, each stacked on the envelope it arrived in and each envelope on a plastic evidence bag. "I've arranged them in the order they seem to have arrived."

Five total. She'd only seen him open four. The first seemed innocuous—simply a letter and, like the envelope, bore the address of *Mine Artiste*. She skimmed the letter. It read like a piece of fan mail; her work was provocative and beautiful, it touched the letter writer, and they couldn't get enough of it, and they really wished she'd held her gallery opening in Dallas rather than Boston. The signature read *Yours*. Nothing else.

Innocuous enough. The next letter had also been addressed to her, and it complained again about her gallery opening and the media coverage. Her fan didn't like how much attention *Her Marine* received, and recommended she work on more classical subject material. Three photographs were included—all seminal works from classical sculptors including Michelangelo.

The third had held the news clippings from Boston. She'd been photographed in two of them—one at the actual gallery opening, and another a headshot her agent had insisted she have in her promotional materials. Every mention of *Her Marine* had been highlighted, and the note attached took her to task for celebrating the military and warmongering and went on at length about her betraying her gift. It seemed a little insane.

It also made her mad.

The fourth envelope contained the photographs. Normal, four-by-six snapshots like those developed from traditional film. Each taken in Boston and all with Liam. A red circle had been drawn around Liam—only there was no letter with it. "What do the red circles mean?"

"Good a question, this man isn't Brody Essex."

"No," she told Foster. "That's Liam Gardiner. He's a banker in Boston. Should I call him?" Proximity to her had already hurt him once. She didn't want this to mean anything else would happen to him.

"Helena is calling him again right now," Damon said. Shannon had forgotten he still had his wife on the phone. His quiet murmurs had blended into the background of her racing heart.

None of this made sense.

"You and Mr. Gardiner seem pretty intimate in this photograph, but nothing is going on between you?" Foster drew her attention to the last picture. It had been taken in the bar at the second hotel she'd moved to after the break-in. They were laughing, and Liam had a hand on her arm.

"No, we're friends."

"They're friends," Logan said from right behind her. "Stop trying to trip her up, she's not a criminal, Foster."

"Sometimes people don't know what they know. They look intimate, and whoever is sending this doesn't like it."

"But there's only red circles. No letter." Which didn't suggest anything positive, by any stretch. Foster backed up a step, and she studied the contents of the fifth envelope—it was another letter, but significantly longer than the first. Three pages longer. Foster had set the pages side by side. It read like an instruction manual, including advice on what projects she should be focusing on, when she should be done, and even the style she should emulate.

Almost ready to label it a crank letter, she paused at the

last three lines.

You need to follow my instructions. I won't offer you another chance to stop debasing yourself. Don't make me regret offering you this one.

It was signed *Always Yours*.

Dread crept through her.

"I'm not a profiler," Foster said, repeating his earlier assertion. "But whoever is sending these thinks they have a personal relationship with you. We're going to run them for prints, and we're going to take a hard look at your life."

No.

"I also think you should come stay with James and I for a few days," Lauren added.

No.

"Or at least on campus at Mike's Place." This from Zach. "We can all keep an eye on you there."

No.

"My work is here, and I have a security system."

Brody had wanted her to install it, and she'd paid good money for one. The loft—everything she worked on was here. When Brody came home, he expected her to be here. "Are you saying you think I'm not safe here?"

Glancing at the men surrounding her, she didn't miss the troubled frowns. Before Foster could say anything, Logan shrugged. "Whoever this freak is, they think they have say in your life."

"The photos say he's stalking you." Lauren said, her tone as sober and serious as her expression. "Honey, I've dealt with stalkers. Some are all hot air, others are different. You're here by yourself...."

"But I live here. I *work* here." If she had to leave.... "These are just letters, and the police have them, and I'll get a camera." God, she didn't want to leave. She wanted to make all of this go away. Fear had been an acid eating away at her soul for too many years. She loved the life she'd built, but she was tired of being hemmed in by all the men. Nudging past

Lauren, she retreated into the kitchen and away from all of them.

"Then one of us can stay here for a while," Damon said. "We can rotate shifts. At least then you're not alone."

All the air in her lungs seemed to back up, and she couldn't get a deep breath. Spots edged her vision, and her heart pounded so loud, surely they could hear it.

"Breathe." Zach ordered and pushed her into a chair and urged her to put her head down between her knees. She tried to do what he said, but the air seemed to rattle in her chest.

"Here." Lauren was suddenly there with a white paper sack from their Chinese carryout. Zach held it up to her face. They wanted her to use it to breathe. Oh, hell, she was having a panic attack. Grasping the bag, she forced her respiration to slow, and the paper crinkled with each inhale and exhale.

"It's going to be okay, Shannon." Zach knelt in front of her. "Just focus on breathing, and we're going to get someone else to stay with you, okay?"

No, it wasn't okay, but how did she explain that? They were only letters. Letters didn't scare her near as much as having some man stay there, and it didn't matter if he happened to be one of Brody's friends.

God. Brody.

If they told him, he'd worry and he was so far away. Pulling the bag away, she panted. "Please don't tell Brody. You can't tell him."

"We're going to tell him, sweetheart," Zach said, giving her a patient and kind look. "He needs to know, but we're going to let him know you're safe and we're taking care of things, too."

"No, he's trying to get through everything so he can come home. He's still over there—where they blow Marines up and shoot them. If he's distracted, he might miss something and then not come home at all." It gave her nightmares even thinking about it. She'd never fooled herself about his job. She'd seen the Marines who'd come home with pieces missing like Rebel or scared like Logan—or even Zach and Logan's wife, Jazz. She'd struggled through her recovery.

A few more weeks and Brody would be away from all the danger. He'd stayed whole and safe so far, she needed him to be that way until he came home.

"We don't have to tell him right away," Lauren offered, when the others remained quiet. The Marines were Brody's friends, his brothers—they'd want to tell him. "We don't," Lauren repeated more firmly. "But you need to take precautions."

"Yeah," Damon said, stepping into her line of sight. "Fine, we can loop Brody in later, but you need someone here with you, or you need to come back to Mike's Place with us." Those were the only two options, and everyone seemed to agree with him.

"Or I can recommend a third idea," Archer Morgan said, entering the conversation for the first time since he'd arrived.

Shannon took another few breaths with the bag and stared at him. "I don't even know who you are."

"A friend, ma'am." He gave her a faint smile. "I'm opening a security firm. We're not off the ground yet, but I already have a team lined up. One of its members would be perfect."

So *he* didn't seem to be offering to do it himself, which helped alleviate some of her panic.

"Katrina?" Foster glanced at his friend.

"Yeah," Morgan nodded. "Katrina Bates. She's ex-Army, former military police, and damn good at what she does." Though he didn't specify what that was. "If you don't want a man here, she can hang out with you."

Heat stung her cheeks at his description—no, she didn't want a *man* here, but she'd been trying to not say the words. It sounded ungrateful and harsh to the men who had shown up because Lauren called.

Zach had risen and backed up a step, even Damon retreated out of her space. The men gave her room to breathe and only Lauren remained. It helped.

"Damn," Zach murmured. "Sorry about that."

"It's okay," she said, hating her own weakness. "I have panic attacks sometimes."

"It's okay, *chère*." Damon told her and Logan echoed the sentiment. "We're all big boys, and we can handle it." But he turned to Morgan and eyed him. "Give me this Katrina Bates' details. We want to check her out before we agree to anything."

They moved away, increasing their distance to her, and Shannon's heart rate slowed. She'd been doing so damn well. Tears burned. Not perfect, but so much better. Now she'd succeeded in making people who were trying to help her feel badly.

"Sweetie, stop." Lauren said, her voice soft and pitched low. "The guys get it, and they aren't mad. They just want to know you're okay. So do I. This is probably a lot of nothing and you get a roommate for a few days...."

Lauren might be a great actress, but she really was a terrible liar.

Chapter Three

*K*atrina Bates turned out to be an ideal roommate. The thirty-something, African-American woman arrived an hour after Archer Morgan recommended her. Sleek and beautiful, she moved on silent feet, and Shannon half-forgot she was there. They had coffee together in the morning, and when Shannon retreated to her sculpting, Katrina worked out in a space she'd cleared and then pulled out a laptop. She even answered the landline. They had a couple of *no caller ID* hang-ups and twice her agent called—the *Her Marine* offer had climbed up to nearly three-quarters of a million dollars, but Shannon remained steadfast in her refusal.

True to his word, Damon arranged for a camera to be installed on her front door, and she could see who came and went. They'd upgraded the security system—including sensors for breaking glass. She'd worried those sensors would be tripped by her chiseling, but so far so good. Companionable silence reigned save for the music, the rush of water and chipping.

The first night Katrina stayed, she'd asked about the sculpting with genuine interest. The second night, she commented on the painstaking process and work. The third, she'd told Shannon stories about her army service. Overall,

Katrina proved friend material, and it didn't take her long to forget why the woman had all but moved into her loft. It didn't hurt that no new letters arrived and Detective Foster hadn't called either.

By the fourth day, they'd settled so soundly into their routine Shannon could focus on the stone. She'd finished the shape of Rebel's head, including his hair, and she worked on his face. This delicate work required a great deal more concentration. Her fingers stung a little as water washed over the stone to clear away the debris. Using a small hammer and chisel, she focused on the shape of one eye, and then the other.

Sweat slicked her back, and her legs were spattered with flecks of stone. She'd dragged her hair up and confined it in a messy bun out of it to try and cool herself off, but not even the air-conditioning could keep up with the energy generated by her muscles. Fatigue wore at her arms by the time she'd finished the nose and mouth, and the sun was setting.

The brutal burn in her shoulders couldn't be ignored any longer, and she finally took a step back and set her tools down. Perched on the edge of a stool, she sagged. Weariness struck, and all she wanted to do was fall into her bed and go to sleep, but she needed a shower first.

"Damn," Katrina said in a low voice. She filled the singular syllable with an element of awe. After crossing the room, she handed Shannon a bottle of water, bless her. The water was icy cold, and she drank it greedily. "I cannot get over this. It didn't have a face this morning, and now.... I mean you can even see the faint dimple in his cheek."

"Thank you," Shannon exhaled the words. Her whole body felt like it had been lit on fire, every muscle in her back and shoulders protesting the length of time she'd held her arms up while performing the careful task of sculpting the face. "I usually do the detail work last, but I wanted to *see* him." The explanation spilled out of her. "I can see it in my mind and in the photographs, but it's different when I find it in the stone."

"I'll say." Katrina stood a foot back, arms folded, her

attention on the sculpture. "You know, when I saw you doing this on the first day, I couldn't figure out how you were ever going to turn a block of gray into a person, and now here he is. That's some serious talent."

Flushing, Shannon ducked her head and finished her water. "I think I'll go take a shower and then I'm going to sleep."

"Eat first, because you skipped lunch today."

"I did?" Had she really? They'd had bagels at breakfast. Shannon'd had a craving, and they'd walked together to her favorite shop a block over to fetch them. After, they returned, ate their bounty and had coffee, and Shannon had went back to her sculpting.

"Go take your shower," Katrina said with a laugh. "I'm going to grill those steaks we picked up. You can eat and then sleep."

Belatedly, it occurred to Shannon that cooking fell well outside the parameters of Katrina's job. "You shouldn't have to feed me, too."

More laughter met the protest, and Katrina pointed her toward the bedroom. "Hell, I need to eat, and trust me, I'm billing Archer for every penny of this."

A cold chill went up her spine. Shannon had to pay for this—and for the first time, she realized she had no idea how much the cost would be. Tossing a smile of gratitude in Katrina's direction, she headed behind the silkscreen divider. Grabbing her cell phone, she turned on the shower to heat up the water before dialing her agent. The call went to voice mail. "Hey, it's Shannon. I need to find out how much the bodyguard business is costing. I didn't think about the daily rates or any of that, and I want to make sure we can pay our end of the bill."

Damon would have been offended if she'd offered to pay him for installing the camera. Zach and Logan, too. But Archer Morgan said he was opening a security office and Katrina worked for him. Shannon agreed because it seemed the best solution, appeased everyone's worries, she didn't have to have a man stay with her, and she didn't have to leave her loft.

But if it bankrupted her in the meanwhile, that didn't help anyone. Putting the phone on the counter, she spared a look at herself in the mirror. *Ugh, mistake.* The bags under her eyes were puffy, her hair was definitely a rat's nest, and her skin actually seemed a little gray itself under all the spatter of debris.

After stripping out of her clothes and pulling the band from her hair, Shannon ducked under the hot spray. It pounded her weary muscles, and she simply stood there for several minutes, letting it sluice away the debris. Sometimes, she felt a lot like the sculptures she created. She had to carve herself back out of the zone and find the woman beneath the obsessed artist.

Frankly, she found being the artist easier. The artist had a purpose and goals and confidence. All of her desire poured into the stone and gave it life. The woman was a mass of contradictions. She hadn't talked to Brody in forever. Was he even back Stateside? At last check-in, he'd traveled inland. First to report to a base then await orders to bring him home. So could he be back? Was he working on finishing up whatever task he needed to do?

She had to stop being stupid. He would call her. Brody didn't have a dishonest bone in his body, never lied to her or strung her along. When he said he would do something, he did it. *But what if he has changed his mind? What if the last couple of years have been too hard on him?* The niggling voice of doubt would not be silenced.

A rumble of thunder rolled over the building, and Shannon shoved her head under the water to soak her hair. They needed the rain. Three years of drought conditions left the landscape yellow and brown. The rain might also bring relief from the heat.

Or transform it into a humid mess.

Either way, thinking about the weather helped distract her

from the longing in her soul. Washing and rinsing her hair helped. Soaping off the last of the gray dirt and scrubbing her sore hands helped. She stared at the blunt, torn nails and scraped skin.

She'd never have smooth, silky hands. The calluses had been well-earned over the years. But they looked like hell. Sighing, she rinsed once more and shut the water off. Being maudlin didn't help anyone. She stepped out and wrapped one towel around her hair and a second around her body when the power flickered once, twice, and then went out entirely.

Crap. On the upside, at least she hadn't been in the shower when it went dark.

"Hang tight," Katrina called. "I'm going to go check the breakers." Thunder boomed outside, louder and a lot closer. Shannon jumped despite knowing the storm had arrived.

"Okay." Thankfully, that came out a great deal more confident than she felt. Gray light filtered through the windows and left the loft in shadows. Shannon toweled off hurriedly. At least she knew where everything was, and she fished out some clean cotton pants and a tank top from the laundry basket—another thing she'd been ignoring since getting home. She'd have to haul some laundry down to the corner and wash a few loads. Dressed, she perched on the edge of her bed and rubbed her hair vigorously. With the power out, Katrina would have to use the back stairs to get to the fuse box.

The power remained off, however, so Shannon settled for combing out her hair. Padding out of the bedroom, she glanced around the studio. The rain lashed at the windows, and lightning brightened the sky. The flickers were damn near blinding and left spots on her vision.

Two plates sat on the counter, loaded with steaks and baked potatoes. When the hell had Katrina baked potatoes? Of course, a bomb could have gone off while Shannon sculpted and she wouldn't notice. Another boom rattled the windows and lightning strobed across the sky. At the open stairwell door, Shannon squinted into the gloom.

"You find it? It might not be us," she called. Sometimes when storms were bad they could knock out power to the whole block. The reclaimed warehouse district hadn't been the best neighborhood before people like she had moved in and started converting the buildings. Old wiring could be tricky in bad weather.

No answer.

Twisting around, Shannon traded her comb for the flashlight stuck to the fridge. Clicking it on, she descended the steps. "Katrina?"

Still no answer.

She reached the first floor and exited the stairwell into the empty warehouse. Someday, she wanted to convert the first floor into a gallery where she could feature her works and other local artists. It would be a great project. Maybe after the showing in Boston she'd have enough money to get a jump-start on that.

Thunder boomed again.

"Katrina?" she called, shining the light across the empty space and then headed to where the fuse box was. She nearly tripped over the woman. Katrina sprawled across the concrete floor. Dropping to her haunches, Shannon touched her neck. A pulse fluttered beneath her fingertips. "Crap, Katrina, are you okay?" Had she tripped over something in the dark?

Struggling to turn her over, Shannon stared at the bloom of red on the woman's chest.

Her eyes fluttered open. "Go," Katrina whispered. "Go now."

But a hard hand covered Shannon's mouth and swallowed her scream. Thick arms came around her, and she flailed as they hauled her backward. Shannon struck at the person grabbing her with the flashlight, but he kept dragging her and then her feet weren't on the ground.

Heart racing, she dissolved into pure panic.

Rain spattered her face, and the chill water snapped her out of the blankness. Jagged lightning sizzled through the air, splitting the darkness in half. Awareness of the precarious nature of her situation hit her. Someone carried her, and she lay upside down over his shoulder. The man moved with purpose.

The world tilted, and she landed on a leather seat. She managed to force her eyes open in time to see the car door shut. Another flash of lightning illuminated the sky and a man in a hoodie, but the backlight transformed him into a harsh slash of a shadow. He climbed into the front seat.

Her wrists were bound, palm-to-palm, with plastic ripcord. She still wore her cotton slacks and tank top. He started the engine. Rain beat on the roof, but beneath the noise and the thunder...she heard him.

Humming.

Sickness swam through her. An image of Katrina flashed through her mind. The lovely woman sprawled on the concrete. Bleeding. He'd shot her. The man had shot her—or stabbed her. It didn't matter. She'd been hurt.

And he was taking Shannon.

The engine.... Dashboard lights added color to the gloom, and the windshield wipers snapped. She rolled against the seat as the car started to move. Move.

The car moved.

Adrenaline flooding her, Shannon twisted on the seat and reached for the door handle. The sound of the latch giving trumpeted through her system like a gift from God. Sitting up abruptly, she swung her legs, then threw herself out of the vehicle before she could think about it. She slammed into the concrete and rolled.

The impact knocked all the wind out of her. Her cheek scraped on the ground. Brakes squealed, and she rolled over to see the vehicle stop. *Get up. Get up and run. Run. Run.*

Somehow, she got her legs under her, and she fled. Not back to the loft—he'd gotten into the loft. She ran for the corner. A coffee house-turned-nightclub occupied a space less than a block away. The thunder boomed, and the rain poured harder.

Run.

Oxygen burned in her lungs, but still she ran, ignoring the way the ground seemed to bite at her feet. She reached the corner. Behind her a car door slammed. Lights swam in her vision, then she raced across the road and another car jerked to a halt. Shannon opened her mouth and screamed for all she was worth, but she didn't stop running.

Ahead of her, the club lights shone like a beacon. Mario, the bouncer, stepped out. His dark scowl turned fierce at the sight of her, then he surged down the street to meet her. "Call the police," she told him, not even caring he had a hold of her arm. "Call them. He shot her. He shot Katrina."

Mario searched the street behind her. "Where?"

"My loft." She panted, even squeezing those two words out hurt. Gulping in another breath, she let Mario shove her into the club. The hostess—Lisa—gasped at the sight of her before rushing out to help. Then Gabe, owner of the club, was there. He was an artist, and they were friends.

They were all friends. But Katrina was back there.

"Hurry," she begged.

"Mario's calling 9-1-1 right now." Lisa wrapped something around Shannon, but it didn't help. She couldn't stop shaking.

She didn't think she would ever stop shaking.

Ninety minutes later, her nightmare continued. She sat in an emergency room cubicle with a nurse cleaning the cuts and scrapes on her arms. They'd rushed Katrina into surgery. Thank God she'd still been alive when the ambulance and the police arrived.

Angry voices rose in the hallway, and one masculine, commanding voice cut through the argument. A moment later, the curtain surrounding her space jerked back. She flinched, she couldn't help it. Even the nurse jumped. They both turned to look at the man framed by the green fabric. Luke Dexter.

Tall, lean and wearing a foreboding expression, he was the kind of man who would normally scare the hell out of her. But more than that, he was Brody's best friend....

Tears filled her eyes and she started to shake all over again.

The nurse hustled and then the blanket she had wrapped around Shannon went away and a warmer one replaced it. "You need to wait outside," the nurse ordered Luke, her tone brooking no objections.

"I will," he said, and his voice gentled from the brusque command. "We're out here waiting for you, Shannon. You're safe."

She gave him a jerky nod. The *we* probably meant the others in Brody's unit; they were like his brothers. He had no other family to speak of. He'd grown up an orphan, bounced around the system until he'd all but run away to join the military at eighteen. Men like Luke, Logan, Damon—they were his family.

"Is Katrina going to be okay?" No one had told her anything since they'd arrived at the hospital.

Luke didn't lie to her. "I don't know. Morgan's heading up to yell at someone on the surgical floor and get details. Her family has been contacted. She was alive when she got to the hospital and alive when they took her into surgery. Those are good things."

"I'm so sorry." God, the damnable quaver in her voice made the words shiver.

"You have nothing to be sorry about," he said. "You were the victim."

Oh, how Shannon hated that word. She huddled into the blanket, wincing as the nurse went to work on her cheek. She'd had some rocks or gravel in her arm—and apparently some in her cheek, too. Everything hurt. Trying to take a mental inventory of the aches and pains proved impossible.

"Foster is here."

As if to confirm Luke's statement, Detective Foster's voice rumbled from beyond the curtain. "Cavanaugh, I need to talk to my witness."

"You can wait." Logan's tone was pure steel.

Luke gave her a gentle smile. "We'll hold the line. You can talk to him when you're ready."

"I should talk to him, though." The trembling in her limbs felt like permanent vibrations. Queasiness swam through her stomach.

"Absolutely," he said, his voice quiet and agreeable. "When you're ready."

The male voices outside rose in argument. The sharp bite of cursing colored the air, and Shannon winced.

"You rest, let the nurse clean you up and the doctor finish his exam. Damon and Helena will be here in fifteen minutes."

"I need you to step out. Now." The nurse walked over to the curtain, and Luke gave her a nod, but his gaze found Shannon's again.

"We're all out here. No one is going to get to you, understood?" At no point did his voice rise or harden. The commanding tone didn't waver, but neither did the kindness. She believed him and, oddly, knowing those Marines were out there did help. The nurse closed the curtain and then returned to Shannon.

"Okay, hon. You've got a lot of bruises and scrapes. We've cleaned those up. But the doctor will want to do some X-rays as well. But I have to ask you, was there any sexual contact related to the attack?"

That did it. Shannon rolled onto her side and threw up.

When Helena arrived, she came with fresh clothes. It took another hour for X-rays and then the doctor checked her over. Thankfully, the nurse never left her, and Helena stayed in the exam room. Once the doctor gave her clearance, Helena helped her dress. Her clothes helped, the news that Katrina survived a gunshot wound to the abdomen helped more.

By the time Helena and Luke escorted her to a small

conference room, Damon waited for them with a large Styrofoam cup of coffee and another container of food. "I don't know if I can eat," she admitted, exhausted.

"You can try, and you should." Damon set her up a place to eat and then backed off. He and Luke took positions at the halfway point in the room. Helena sat next to her. Only after the detective arrived did Shannon realize they'd all put themselves between her and the cops.

"Miss Fabray," Detective Foster greeted her. "I am sorry for what happened and sorrier that we need to question you tonight. But we need details, as much as you can remember about what happened."

She tried to recount it as best she could—from the moment the power went off to when she threw herself out of the car. "Then I ran up the road. There's a club and I knew it would be open...and Mario heard me and got me in out of the rain."

"Did you get a good look at the man who took you?" Foster recorded her statement, and Shannon shook her head.

"It was dark." An image flashed through her mind. The lightning splitting the sky, the dark shadow looming over her. "He had a hoodie on. I think. It looked like one."

"Okay, what about the car?"

Again, she shook her head. "I found Katrina...she was still awake. She told me to go, to run. But then he grabbed me." A shudder wracked her, and she put down the coffee cup before she dropped it. "He had a hand over my mouth and...." It all went blurry after that. A sick feeling surged through her stomach.

"I fought.... I hit him with the flashlight. I think I dropped it. But he didn't let me go and then I was over his shoulder and it was raining." Her wrists had been bound. She rubbed at them. The red marks were still livid and promised to bruise. "Then he dropped me in the car."

Foster studied her. "But he didn't lock you in?"

"I guess not. I heard the engine start and the car started to move. I reached for the door, and it opened. All I thought about at that point was getting away."

"Did he chase you?"

"I don't know." She hadn't looked back. The car had stopped. But she'd gotten herself up and ran. "I just wanted to get away."

"You ran for the club and not back to your loft...."

"He'd already gotten in there, and Katrina was hurt. I didn't want to take him back to her...and I wanted to get away." He'd touched her. He'd carried her, and something in the car—when the engine started—ramped up her fear. It had snapped her out of the fugue that had left her bound and let her run.

"So, you ran to the club. How about once you were there? Did you see anyone on the street behind you?"

Mario had rushed out to meet her. She'd screamed. "I don't know. I don't think so. I was inside, and Lisa put something around me. Mario watched the door and then the cops came and the ambulance.... I made them go to my place for Katrina."

"You're doing great, Miss Fabray. I need you to think back again to the moment you were grabbed. Did he say anything?"

Had he? The images jumbled together. A hand over her mouth. A hard arm locking around her. Being lifted off the ground. Hitting him to no avail. Then...nothing. God, why couldn't she remember what happened between when he grabbed her and when she woke over his shoulder?

How long had it lasted? She didn't know, and the doctors had run a rape kit. Humiliation slithered through her, and she shook her head. Her mind kept jerking back to the moment the car started, and her skin crawled.

"Anything he may have said. It could be one word?" Foster pressed, and the quaking in Shannon's hands turned into shivering all over. She folded her arms. Another negative response. "Miss Fabray, I understand this is hard. But you're really close to it right now, little details can fade in a day or two. Maybe you smelled something? On him? In the car? You said it was a four-door, right?"

"Yes. But I don't know anything else. It was a car, it had doors. He was a man. He grabbed me. I woke up over his shoulder and my wrists were tied with one of those plastic zip cords. He dumped me in the backseat hard enough that I bounced and then he slammed the door. The rain was coming down, and there was thunder and lightning, and he started the engine...all I wanted to do was get away."

The detective nodded. "Let's go back to before the lights went out. What did you do?"

"I took a shower. I'd been sculpting, working on a new piece. I was tired and filthy. I wanted to go take a shower, and Katrina said she'd grill some steaks and we could eat and then I could sleep." It had been a normal day—as normal as her days had been since the bodyguard moved in.

"What about the rest of your day? Anyone come by? Any new letters?"

"No." She rubbed her face. "I would have told you if I received any. Is this the same person?"

"We're going to investigate, and hopefully, Miss Bates can give us more information when she wakes up. Until then, let's go back over this again...."

Oh, God. She did not want to do this again. "I don't know anything else. They did something with my fingernails—" Not that she had any. She didn't remember touching his skin, only the feeling of his hand on her mouth. The way he squeezed her and then the panic followed by nothingness until the rain struck her outside.

She hated not remembering.

"I understand this is difficult...." But Detective Foster trailed off, and Shannon glanced up to find Luke's hand raised.

"Enough. She told you what she remembers. James can talk to her tomorrow or the day after or whenever she is ready, and see if she can remember more. But we're done here. We're taking her home."

"Not to the loft. I've got my crime scene techs there right now."

Shannon would throw up again. All those people all over her place—and that man. And Katrina's blood.

"We're taking her to Allen." Luke held out a card. "You want to talk to her, call me first."

"Or me," Helena said, speaking for the first time. "I also want copies of the reports you have on those letters and a statement regarding the investigation."

Foster agreed with them, and Shannon faded out of the conversation. Nothing made sense. The break-in, the letters, and tonight...tonight the man had shot Katrina.

"Shannon." Luke knelt next to her seat. "This is going to be okay, sweetheart. We're taking you back to Mike's Place. You'll stay with Rebecca and I tonight."

She'd had a bodyguard at her loft, and she'd been shot. What if...? "No, if the guy comes back, I don't want you or Rebecca to be hurt."

One hand on the table and the other on the arm of her chair, he was careful not to touch her, but his expression didn't soften. "I've got guys locking the campus down, and we're doubling security. I've also asked anyone who isn't living on campus currently to come in and rotate a shift. You're going to be surrounded by Marines, sweetheart. No one is going to touch you again. Okay?"

It sounded so good.

"Now, is there anything we can get you before we go?"

Brody.

She wanted Brody. But she couldn't have him.

Chapter Four

"*It's Shannon, she was attacked...*"

From the moment Luke said the words, anger pooled in the pit of Brody's belly before rising and growing caustic in the back of his throat. Not only had she been attacked, but someone had tried to kidnap her and he'd shot another woman in the process. The woman survived, but she would be in the hospital for the foreseeable future. Some primal part of Brody had shut down his emotional responses, dug in, and crouched to wait as the rest of him listened to Luke's assessment.

Shannon's loft a crime scene. They'd taken her back to Mike's Place. Most of Brody's former unit worked or lived at the veteran's rehabilitation center. The sprawling complex had grown in the three years since it had opened and continued to expand. He'd joked once about how it had the feel of living on a base—it also had the security of one. Luke said he'd called in all available men, they had a rotating guard working and constant monitoring.

Whoever the fucktard was that had gone after Shannon wouldn't get near her again. The anger boiling in his belly began to sizzle beneath the ice of his control. The cops, it seemed, had no leads.

And there was more.

Brody had to stand in Coms, surrounded by others doing their jobs, and keep his expression clean of reaction as Luke detailed Shannon's hotel break-in, the letters, the assessment from the cops—at least the detective in charge of her case was a former Marine even if Brody didn't recognize the name—and another summation of the attempted kidnapping. As if aware Brody needed to know, he repeated Shannon's condition—fine physically, aside from bumps, bruises, and scrapes she'd gotten while throwing herself out of a moving car.

For fuck's sake.... Brody clenched his fist and resisted the urge to slam it against the wall. Physically fine she might be, but what about emotionally and mentally? She'd had issues for years, thanks to some jackass raping her in college. Emotional wounds had sealed the infection in with thick scar tissue.

She'd started to heal, finally. And now this.

"Is she there now?" The first question he allowed himself to ask.

"She's asleep," Luke said. Of course. It was mid-day in Afghanistan and that meant it was still the middle of the night in Dallas. "James had one of the doctors prescribe something for her. She seemed to be doing okay until we got back here."

Seemed to be translated to *not at all*. Poise and control had driven Shannon on a date with a stranger two years before. The need to reclaim her desire and control her passion being fuel for the fire. Yes, she'd said it had to do with her art, but beneath it all, she was a lonely, hurt woman who wanted to be more. Brody always counted himself fucking fortunate to be the man she'd met. She'd needed *him,* and he'd given her what she needed.

Leaving her had been hard, they'd had a few days in Italy and a few Skype calls to tide him over. She sent him letters— real honest-to-God letters—and emails, always letting him know he had someone waiting. For the first time since he'd enlisted, someone at home gave two shits if he made it back or not.

And the reality of it was, he'd been marking the time till he went home to her permanently.

"Brody," Luke's voice reminded him they were still on the phone. "We've got this."

No. They really didn't. "Thank you, sir." But he couldn't comment, not when he could be overheard. What he needed were his orders, so he could get the fuck out of the armpit of hell and home—to her, where he belonged.

His former captain went quiet for a long moment then asked, "Your orders come in yet?"

"No." No, he still waited. It could be an hour or a month. Though scuttlebutt suggested the base commander had a mission for his team that could send them back out.

"Hang in there, you'll be Stateside soon. Till then, we've got your girl, and we're going to keep her safe." What he didn't say was the underlying order in those words. Trust him. Trust his brothers to take care of his girl. They could keep her safe.

He did trust them to protect her—physically. But she'd hide the rest from them. It was what she did. *She had to have been scared out of her mind....*

The watch commander entered the room, and he gave Brody an assessing look. Time to get off the phone. "Keep me in the loop, Luke."

"I will." Without much else to say, they disconnected the call. Leaving Coms, he headed for the base commander's office. Willis was a good man and a tough colonel. He'd been with the first boots on the ground in the first Iraq War and the second, and in Afghanistan nearly as long as the first two assignments put together.

Twenty minutes of cooling his heels later, he had his answer. No orders were forthcoming, and no word on when they might be. Ukrainian politics were hot. Crimea was hot. Africa was always fucking hot. Now, the Far East might also be heating up. Facts were facts.

His orders were coming, but where they were sending him...remained open for debate.

Home.

Shannon needed him at home. He needed to be at home. *Fuck*.... Brody had too many years of training and practice at controlling his expression and body language. He bypassed his quarters and headed for the gym. No fancy equipment, but weight training kept him in shape and sane when he had nothing else to do. Guard duty would be fucking preferable to the waiting he'd engaged in since typing up his last report.

A dozen men were in the various stages of working out. Several paused to salute, and he waved them off. Not bothering to change, he headed straight toward Jennings and Royce. The pair of sergeants spotted him and set their weights aside to hit attention before he arrived.

"At ease," he said, keeping his voice low and conversational. The chance to be overheard existed, but he needed their specialized skills, and they had a better chance of providing him with what he needed out in the open rather than behind closed doors. "Explain to me the swiftest way out country."

"Sir?" Royce reached for the pair of thirty-pounders he'd been using for biceps curls and resumed his routine, but his attention was on Brody.

"I was clear with the order."

He'd led the fast response team for nearly two years. His ability to make decisions on the fly, task resources, implement and see them carried out were part of why he was an effective leader. Every member of his team served a similar purpose. Under heavy fire, questioning a decision could get the whole team killed. They were a well-oiled machine, and he'd never had a problem trusting his life—now his career—to these men.

Jennings claimed a pair of weights and joined Royce with a set of curls. "Package size, sir?"

"About six foot two, two hundred and ten pounds." The sergeants had racked up a tidy sum with a sideline business of bringing in special order supplies for the men—everything from cigarettes to porn. He'd even heard a rumor about bacon bits at one point. They didn't deal in illegal substances—

although pork products were not shipped in by the military in adherence to local laws. They'd also helped ensure packages were sent back to the states, speedier than they might have made it otherwise. All of it tap-danced on the letter of the law, but nothing that would get them more than a restriction in privileges.

And to his knowledge, they'd never allowed it to interfere with their assignments. If he needed water in the middle of the desert, these were the two he would go to.

Hell, they were the two he'd used. The two men glanced at each other and continued to pump iron. Biceps curls finished, they switched to hammer presses. What few but those who'd worked closely with Jennings and Royce realized were the two men rarely communicated aloud. They could convey a wealth of information via a simple glance the other understood.

"Tricky," Jennings said before setting his weights back on the stack. "But not impossible. What's our operational time frame?"

Until that moment, he hadn't realized how committed to the choice he'd become. Shannon needed him Stateside. His orders weren't forthcoming. "As soon as possible."

Neither man commented on the illegality of his choice or the violation of orders. The moment he stepped foot outside the gates, he would be AWOL. At the very least, he would receive disciplinary action and, at worst, a full-blown court martial that might land him in prison.

All acceptable risks as long as he completed his mission and Shannon was safe.

Royce put away his own weights and picked up a towel to sling around his neck. "Documentation?"

"Enough to get me out of here." Here being Afghanistan. Kabul was the closest civilian airport. He certainly couldn't use military transport...could he?

The men exchanged another long, silent exchange and then Jennings nodded curtly. "Two hours. One bag. Northeast gate."

Trusting his men, he nodded. They straightened with a salute, and he returned the same then left them to head to his quarters. He didn't need much, so the one-bag requirement wouldn't be a problem.

Some fifteen hours later, Brody boarded a plane in Paris that would carry him directly to Dallas. The flights cost a small fortune, but he had a hell of a lot of money in the bank he'd never used. Years of not owning a house or needing to buy a vehicle, and eating on military dime had left him with a nice nest egg. Now was as good to use the cash. Jennings and Royce had given him papers allowing him to board a flight from Kabul to Istanbul via a Turkish airline; from there he boarded Air France to Paris. Using his military ID would have gotten him cheaper seats and made tracking him easier, so he simply booked it as a civilian.

The minute he'd exited Camp Leatherneck aboard a supply truck carrying him Kabul, he'd been AWOL. Being out of uniform was the least of his worries. Royce and Jennings promised to cover him for as long as possible. Neither man needed to do it, he didn't expect it, and ordered them not to compromise their own careers.

After passing his ticket and passport to the boarding agent, he waited while she scanned the first and gave a bored glance at the second. Security had tightened at all airports since 9/11, but she was the last stage before boarding a flight. He felt it a safe bet if a person had reached this point, they'd already been vetted by security.

On board, he put his bag in an overhead compartment and took his seat. Once the last passenger boarded and the compartment secured, the flight was only half full. Brody sat alone in his row. That suited him fine.

He didn't relax until the flight took off, but once they reached a cruising altitude, he leaned his head back. His training let him sleep anywhere, and he could do nothing until he arrived in Dallas, so he slept. The stewardess woke him with a light touch an hour out from arrival.

In the bathroom, he washed his face and grimaced at the stubble. The stewardess delivered coffee and orange juice along with a boxed breakfast. He ate and drank methodically and tasted nothing. A little over twenty-seven hours since Luke's call. Once he cleared customs, he would be back on U.S. soil and on his way to Shannon.

As soon as the plane touched ground, he switched his cell phone on and sent a text message. His one duffle bag earned him a second look from the customs agent, but Brody passed over his military ID, and her expression relaxed, her manner taking on one of sympathy. "Home on leave?"

"Yes." Unofficial and unapproved, but definitely on leave to take care of Shannon's problem. Then he could face whatever discipline the Corps meted out.

"Well, welcome home." She passed him his passport and ID card and waved him through. Ten minutes later, he walked out the front doors and took his first full breath of honest-to-God American air in twenty-four months. The heat and humidity slapped at him, but he drank in the feeling greedily. A black truck cruised up to the curb and idled. "Your leave couldn't have happened at a better time," Damon said by way of greeting.

Not bothering to waste his breath—or correct Damon's assumption—Brody had the passenger door open and tossed his bag into the back seat of the four-door cab, before climbing in. "Thanks for the ride."

Better for everyone if they didn't know. That way they couldn't face anything resembling aiding and abetting charges. If they were questioned, they could all answer honestly—they hadn't known. His brothers wouldn't alert the authorities. No, they wouldn't. Still, he refused to involve them any more than he had to. This was on him.

"You're welcome. Damn good to see you." Damon gave him a tight smile and merged into the traffic flow.

"You, too. Tell me what you know." On a clock now, he knew it would only be a matter of when his AWOL was reported, not if. NCIS would open a case file and they would start searching.

If he were them, Dallas would be the first place he looked, too.

Though he'd maintained his calm throughout the long series of flights home, impatience left Brody edgy on the drive through heavy mid-day Dallas traffic. His internal clock continued to tick like a time bomb. Damon caught him up on everything since Luke's phone call.

Shannon was in a third floor apartment on the campus. Her neighbors on either side were retired Special Forces who also worked as physical therapists. No one in her building nursed an injury, and they had someone on watch twenty-four-seven. While not ideal, they'd done their best on short notice.

Damon didn't say anything specific, but worry coated his voice when he mentioned her name.

"She hates everything about the set up, doesn't she?" Brody drummed his fingers. Twenty-seven hours and thirty-eight minutes since Luke's call and he'd gone AWOL, traveled thousands of miles, kept his cool, and if they didn't fucking get out of this traffic, he'd lose his shit.

"Not going to lie, she pretty much shut down after we got her set up. Most of us...the guys are keeping our distance. She made it pretty clear she didn't want to be in close quarters, and Doc spent five minutes with her and put a call through to one of the physicians. Might have been nice to have a heads up about the PTSD." Damon didn't criticize, but he didn't pull his punches either.

"It shouldn't have been an issue." Not for them. Shannon worked with her statues and she'd been getting better. She spent time with Liam. He'd never met the man and he could fucking hug him, because Liam had helped with Shannon's confidence. She'd actually considered staying at his townhouse before ultimately electing to stay in a hotel. No excuses as to why, but with all the other changes and the travel, she thought better to have a bolthole.

A decision she based on recognizing her *needs* and it had taken strength to be objective about it. He'd been so fucking proud of her.

And then this happens.

When he got his hands around this chicken-livered piece of shit, he planned to cut his fucking intestines out and feed them to him while the man was still alive.

"Yeah," Damon said, and judgment etched a hard line beneath the words. "Should have, would have, could have. We didn't *know,* and we scared the ever-loving fuck out of her. Even keeping our distance isn't helping because we can't keep our distance."

Brody accepted the blame. Shannon had been in the States, safe at home. No one should have had anything in for her—least of all some sick fuck sending her nasty letters and trying to kidnap her. He wanted to know who, he didn't really care why. The why didn't matter. The who did. As someone who specialized in fast response, all he needed was a target. Eliminate the target, eliminate the problem, and make his girl safe again.

That was his priority now, but to Damon all he said was, "Sorry, man." From the corner of his eye, he caught Damon's nod. They didn't need a lot of words. "What about Bates?" He'd never met the woman, never heard of her before now, but he owed her. She'd taken a bullet for Shannon.

"Gut wound. Ugly as fuck, but the docs all said she'll pull through. She's in ICU, and Morgan has two of his guys watching over her in case the asshole tries to take another shot. She might be able to ID him." What he didn't have to add was that she hadn't woken up to confirm or deny the supposition. Finally, they were off the highway and the landscape gave way to the green vista he recalled from his last visit to the campus.

Damon waved to a man at the gate, and it lifted while they

were still approaching. The addition of a security gate was new. But the facility continued to grow. He'd received regular updates from all of his brothers here. They'd added new buildings, bought land across the street, and if the scuttlebutt was true, they were building single-family homes and more. Luke Dexter seemed to be taking over the town of Allen, one square mile at a time.

What little amusement he found in the thought was fleeting as Damon drove up the long drive and then took the exit heading into a private parking area. As soon as he put the truck in a parking spot, Brody exited with his bag in hand. "Apartment number?"

"307." Brody was on the move when Damon called after him. "We're here if you need us."

"Thanks," he called back over his shoulder, but didn't slow his pace. He spotted the guard easily enough, and a second one patrolling the green belt. Cameras were placed every thirty yards or so.

Yes, Luke had beefed up his security, and it appeared too precise to be a recent thing. Taking the stairs two at a time, Brody made a mental note to talk to him about it later. The door to 305 opened, and a man stepped out to block his path—Special Forces babysitter number one. He had his cell phone to his ear, and he seemed to be listening for a moment, then he nodded to Brody and backed into his apartment.

Damon called to let them know of his approach most likely, but he didn't slow his pace. At 307, he paused. He needed to have his shit under control when he saw her. The last thing she needed was a caveman treatment or worse, the surge of predatory violence rolling through his blood. Thirty seconds, he counted off in his head before he knocked twice. "Shannon?" Because she didn't need to be afraid for even a second about who waited on the other side the knock. "I'm here, babe."

The door locks tumbled—one, two, and finally a chain rattled before the door opened wide. She stood in front of him, her amber eyes wide and wild in the paleness of her face. Her long hair hung all around her, shining as though she'd brushed it over and over again—a habit she had when truly nervous or trying to work something through. Either sculpting or brushing her hair, and she didn't have her tools here.

A red, angry scrape marred her cheek, and darker shadows bruised the underside of her eyes, but she was still the most beautiful woman in the world to him. His heart felt like it strangled inside, and he gave her a moment to accept his presence, but she moved, rushing forward, and he opened his arms and caught her.

He was home.

Holding her, Brody closed his eyes and drew in a deep breath. He'd not really let himself a moment since the phone call. The only thing that mattered had been getting to her. Slowly, he became aware of everything—how light she felt in his arms, the way her curves pressed to him, and the silken rainfall of her hair brushing on his skin.

"I'm going to carry you inside," he told her in a rough voice.

"Okay." Her voice muffled against his throat. Her fingers dug into his shoulders, her grip tightening. From thousands of miles away, it was easy to forget her physical strength. But he'd seen her carve life from stone, hewing away the excess with skill and patience, until she transformed a rock into a work of art.

Carrying her inside, he dropped his bag on the floor and closed the door with his boot heel. With a twist, he turned the locks and then carried her over to the sofa. Like most of the apartments at Mike's Place, this one had to have been pre-furnished. He'd stayed in a similar one when he'd visited two years before. The layout was straightforward and simple: living room, kitchen, a short hallway to the one or two bedrooms, and a bathroom.

For the time being, Brody ignored all of it to sit on the sofa and cradle Shannon in his lap. She shuddered, and he wanted to rub her back, but he needed to get a good look at her injuries.

"I can't believe you're here," she said and lifted her head. Tears shimmered within the amber of her eyes, and she cupped his face in her palms. The bristle on his cheeks had to scratch her hands, but she didn't pull away. A hand-shaped bruise stretched from above her lip to her chin and across her jaw. Bluish-black circles ringed her wrists.

The shirt she wore hung off one shoulder, and he couldn't miss the bluish-black bruise and red, raw skin. Luke had said she'd thrown herself out of a moving car. He catalogued every mark on her.

"How are your ribs, sweetheart?" Wanting to crush her to him, he kept his touch light to avoid hurting her further.

"Sore." She retreated some, shifting on his lap. Brody kept his arms loose enough so she wouldn't feel trapped, but he adjusted her position so she didn't sit right across his cock because it didn't seem to give a damn about her bruises—only that she was touching him. "Nothing's broken. They did two sets of X-rays."

That was something. Hand raised, he caught a long tendril of her hair and looped it around his finger. "I see the scrapes and the bruises...did he touch you anywhere else?" Damon hadn't mentioned a rape nor had Luke.

"No." Despite the quick reply and headshake, she couldn't disguise the quake in her words or the way her mouth turned down. "They ran a rape kit at the hospital. But I wasn't unconscious for that long, and my pants were still on...this time."

Quiet rage at the bastard itched beneath his skin, and he gave her hair a light tug until she met his gaze. "This is not what happened to you in college." The incident had affected her for years, worsened by her inability to recall what happened exactly. It had battered her self-esteem and confidence, and she'd let herself become isolated from even experimenting with dating. The loss of passion had sent her in his direction in the first place via a service pairing consenting adults for a one-night stand.

And once again, he thanked God they'd been paired together.

"I know, but...."

"No buts." He firmed the conviction in his voice. If she believed nothing else, she had to believe this. "Whoever this"—*jackass-no-balls-son-of-a-bitch*—"person is, we know *exactly* what happened."

Unease and doubt worked over her face, and she bit her lower lip. "But it is kind of like that...."

Not doubting her, he smoothed a hand over her hair. She was real, in his lap, and he could touch her. He needed to remind himself of the fact. "How?"

"Because I don't know why." The words exploded out of her. "Why would someone shoot Katrina? Why...why take me? I haven't done anything."

The bruises went deeper than the surface of her skin, and they'd opened older wounds in her soul. "He's an asshole."

"Brody...." Laughter sparked beneath the exhaustion and tears.

"What?" He raised his eyebrows. "Not a harsh enough word?"

Her weak smile grew. Eyes closed, she leaned into him and rubbed her uninjured cheek to his. Cupping the back of her head, he held her there. The sweet vanilla of her scent had haunted him overseas. He'd always caught a whiff of it on the letters she sent, an elusive tease and reminder of what he missed.

Today, however, she had a bite to her scent—something citrus, clean and fresh, but wholly Shannon. "I missed you." He wanted to hold her like this forever, and he couldn't. Not until he'd dealt with whomever was intent on taking away her freedom and sense of security.

"Me, too," she said with a husky tone that sent all of his blood rushing south. Some women went overboard to be sexy with revealing clothes, cosmetics, perfumes, and attitude. She needed none of those things. With a jerk, she leaned back and worried her lower lip. "You probably want a shower and something to eat. I don't even know how long you've been traveling."

When she would have scooted out of his lap, he kept her still. "I can get all those things. Right now, I just want to hold you." Needed to hold her. Needed to reassure himself of her safety. "And to tell you how proud I am of you." Until he'd said the words aloud, he hadn't realized how proud he truly was, and how much he wanted her to know it.

"For what?" Her brows drew together in confusion, but she softened at his refusal to let her escape. If she'd really wanted to get away from him, he'd never make her stay in place. Her adorable frown held question and doubt, not fear. Choking off the urge to carry her off to her borrowed bed so he could inspect every silken inch of her body, he fisted her hair so he could brush a kiss across her lower lip.

"For getting away from him, sweetheart. You kept your head, you got out of the car, and you went toward people. You didn't freeze up or let the panic hold you captive."

And just like that, her expression fell like a dark cloud blotted out the sun. She dropped her eyes to stare at his chest. "But I did...when I found Katrina on the ground. There was all this blood and then he grabbed me." She shuddered, and her breathing went shallow and reedy. The rattle of it pained him, and he forced his white-knuckled grip to loosen and release her hair.

"You're safe, Shannon." The bastard wouldn't touch her again.

"I should have been safe then, Katrina Bates was former army, and an MP, and she had all this great experience. She was—"

"Is."

She gave a little jerk as though a bullet struck her, and her lashes swept up to reveal her wild, sad eyes. "What?"

"You keep saying what Bates was...she still is. She's alive."
Semantics, maybe, but he worked with what he had. Bates
lived. "Present tense, sweetheart."

"He shot her."

"I know." Whether he'd intended to shoot Shannon or not
haunted Brody. Had he shot Bates because she'd been in his
way? Or had he believed her to be Shannon herself? Had her
descent surprised him? Or had taking her been his plan all
along?

"He grabbed me after I turned her over. She told me to go,
to run." The last came out on a strangled note sounding as if
she'd run out of air. Shifting his grip, he placed two fingers
against her throat. Terror stampeded through the mad beat of
her pulse, and fear echoed in the dilation of her eyes. "I
froze.... I wanted to help her, and I froze. Then he grabbed me.
I tried to fight, Brody, I promise, I wanted to and then I
just...." Her mouth went from tight and white to trembling.

She'd locked up. The body had two responses to danger,
fight or flight. Shannon had gone into flight and shut down. It
happened. He'd seen it happen to trained Marines in the field.
Sometimes survival overwhelmed every other thought, and
her mind couldn't process the fear. "It's okay, sweetheart.
You're not there anymore. He doesn't have you. You did get
away."

Her hands went to his shirt, opening and closing, as she
fisted the fabric.

"You got away." Repeating the phrase, over and over, he
waited the storm out until finally, he said, "Tell me you hear
me."

Slowly, too slowly, her gaze tracked back up to meet his.
The pupils were still fat and dark and threatening to swallow
her irises, but they flickered, tightening for a moment. "I got
away. I ran up the street to the club on the corner. I told you
about it—Lisa and Mario—I eat there sometimes."

"You did." He knew his expression was encouraging, he'd
learned how to keep his own feelings off his face a long time

before. Men needed the man who gave the orders to project confidence and calm. The world could be erupting beneath his feet, and he could maintain his calm. It didn't matter he wanted to beat his fists bloody on the son of a bitch who put that hitching note of alarm in her voice or painted her soft eyes in shadows. Shannon didn't need his fury.

She needed calm. She needed him to believe in her. He had all of that and more to give.

"It was a good choice." An amazing one. Had she gone back into her loft, the bastard could have cornered her. If she'd gone the other way on the street, she would have gone deeper into the reclaimed warehouse district. No, she'd fled directly toward witnesses, and the coward who'd try to steal her hadn't followed her into the light. "The best choice. *You* saved Bates, too."

The tears trembling on her lashes dropped, and her breathing deepened on a gasp. "No, Mario called the police...and the ambulance."

"Maybe he did, fine. He couldn't have if you hadn't fought. If you hadn't won...."

"I didn't win."

Fight flared in her, and Brody bit back a smile. Yes, she had.

"He tried to kill Katrina. He tried to take you. He failed at both." Brody raised his brows. "Unless I missed something, you won."

Her mouth opened as though to refute his statement, and then she closed it and shook her head.

"No? I didn't miss anything?" He brushed his thumb down her unwounded cheek.

"No. I guess I didn't think of getting away as winning."

"Your survival is a win in my book. You won the first battle, sweetheart."

And he would win the war.

Chapter Five

They'd sat together for the better part of an hour when Shannon sent him off to shower. He promised her they'd eat, talk, and then figure out what to do. The last thing he wanted was to leave her alone, but considering her condition, he didn't feel right about inviting her into the shower either. His body had no such protests, but fortunately he didn't think with his cock most of the time.

Not that his cock gave a damn about his opinion. Under the hot spray, need continued to thrum through his veins. Probably because the shower had her shampoo and conditioner. He went with the former and skipped the latter. He tried to get some semblance of order to his thoughts while he showered.

Calling the detective in charge of her case scored high on his list. So was reaching out to Archer Morgan. Morgan had assigned Bates to watch over Shannon. Checking with the hospital had to go on his list because guilt over what happened to the woman would continue to eat Shannon alive on the inside. Assigning each task a priority, he considered the haunted expression on her face. He couldn't escape it no matter what he focused on. Tomorrow, they would attack her problem head on. A planned offense provided her with the best defense.

Tonight...tonight was about being around her. Getting her to laugh, to smile, and to relax. Harder to accomplish when all he could see was how perfectly fuckable she was—the bruises and scrapes didn't do a damn thing to diminish how attractive he found her. Marks of survival. The dead weren't bruised.

They were just dead.

The ache in his balls and the stiffness of his erection were becoming downright painful. He cranked the water from hot to ice cold and hissed out a breath. Unfortunately, even that took a few minutes to be effective. By the time he'd gotten his need leashed, his skin probably looked blue. After shutting the water off, he stepped out of the shower and grabbed a towel.

He'd left the bathroom and bedroom doors open so he could hear her—yes, they were at Mike's Place and security was just outside the apartment, but he wanted to *know* she was all right. Toweling off briskly, he paused at the sound of the first lock tumbler. Alarm rang through his system. Slinging the towel around his hips, he headed straight for the front door.

"Thank you," Shannon said as she swung the door inward, but Brody cut in front of her to intercept the delivery of two large pizza boxes and a six-pack of beer. To his credit, the man's eyes widened and he retreated a step.

"All paid for man." He thrust the stuff forward, and Brody barely caught the boxes before the man about pissed himself to back off and head for the stairs. Balancing the pizzas and beer, Brody closed and locked the door before rounding to meet Shannon's wide eyes.

"Don't open the door again. Not when you're alone."

"I called the gate like I was supposed to when I ordered the pizza." The explanation spilled out of her in a rush. "You were in the shower, and I thought you deserved something to celebrate being home."

"I don't want to celebrate." The words came out harsher than intended.

Shannon's lips compressed, and her expression closed off. Exhaling a breath, he motioned her into the kitchen and prowled after her. Once in there, he set the boxes and the beer on the counter. She had no idea of his status, only that he'd come home. And he'd have to fucking apologize for yelling at her.

Instead of shutting down, however, she folded her arms and lifted her chin. Rebellion, not retreat, flared in her eyes. "Well, maybe I wanted to celebrate."

The stubborn set of her mouth, and the anger in her expression eradicated all the work the cold shower had done. "Shannon...."

"I wasn't *asking* you."

She wasn't, Brody realized, and the restlessness pumped through his system, and his anger was the first to fall. "I see."

"Do you?" Marching toward him, she raised her chin and tilted her head. As long-limbed and gorgeous as she was, he still stood taller. The hollows in her cheeks and the bruises on her face infuriated him—but her spirit? It glowed fiercely and lit her up from the inside. "I'm not a *victim*. Everyone else is treating me like a victim. You *didn't*."

No, he hadn't. Because his Shannon was a fighter, and she'd fought. She'd won. Pride loosened fear's grip on his heart. In the bathroom, when he'd heard the door, terror seized him. He would not allow harm to strike her again. Not when he could prevent it.

"I don't see you as a victim," he said, and she was close enough to touch. To drag to him and to kiss her until the only thing she could touch, taste, or feel was him.

"Don't you?" Challenge slammed through the two words. "Could have fooled me. Get dressed and have your damn beer and eat your pizza or don't...I'll have them."

He narrowed his eyes at the command. "Go ahead." He leaned against the kitchen doorframe, not allowing her to leave. "Eat."

"Maybe I'm not hungry." Defiance etched into every

muscle. Her shoulders were back, her chin raised, cheeks flushed. The fresh wash of pink chased away the haunting paleness.

No, she just didn't like the fact he pushed back. He'd pushed her to demand what she wanted, to take it. The scare she'd experienced had rattled her badly, and based on Damon's summary and her declaration, everyone had treated her fragility and fear, enhancing them. At the moment, Brody was less concerned about her fear than her bravado.

He'd never discourage her, and he admired her strength, but.... "You're hungry. You haven't been eating well."

"How the hell do you know what I'm doing? You weren't *here*." God, she was beautiful when she stopped behaving as though someone kicked her puppy. Maybe he was responsible—he took pride in the ferocity of her tone and the bite in her gaze.

"So, you weren't exhausted from your gallery opening? A little shocky from the break-in and worn out from being surrounded by people?" He took a step toward her, and she held her ground. *Good girl. Push back.* "You didn't lock yourself in your loft and dive back into your work? Losing yourself in sculpting?" He closed the distance between them. "So much so you didn't check your mail, and if Lauren hadn't been a pushy friend, you wouldn't have known some crazy jackass was sending you letters? Or maybe you ate after someone dragged you out of your place and tossed you in a car and the only way you could escape involved falling out of a moving vehicle?"

For a split second, her lower lip trembled, but his girl had spunk in her, and she sucked in a deep breath. He stood practically on top of her now, and she slapped her hand to his chest to halt his progress. The sting couldn't compete with the sizzle of contact. Two years had wrought more changes in her than he'd been privy to, though he'd suspected from the way she phrased sentences or spoke.

"You're being an ass," she said and pushed—not that she

could move him. The simple act of trying, of standing up for herself, and her willingness to show him her anger...damn, it was the sexiest thing he'd ever seen.

"Yes, I am." He covered her hand and held it to his skin. Electricity rippled through him, and all his good intentions from earlier shattered in the wake of the simple contact. "But I like your ass in one piece. You can be pissed. You can yell at me. You can throw things at me. I'm game for all of it. But you will do as you're told in this one area until I know you're safe."

Her mouth slackened and formed a simple *O*. "I would never throw anything at you."

"No? Damn. Guess I'll have to work harder." And he slammed his mouth down on hers, giving into the desire eating away at him since she'd opened the door.

His mouth took hers, claimed her. Nothing soft or tentative interrupted his kiss. He wrapped his arms around her, drawing her to his chest and she clung to him. Where their tongues met, it felt like a dance and a surrender. She'd waited for this kiss—waited over a year. Months of aching, hoping, and praying he would come home, be safe and in one piece. Suddenly he was there, his mouth on hers, surrounding her with protection and desire and perfection.

The muscles under her hands were hard and tense. He didn't strain to lift her off the ground, and she was suddenly weightless, supported utterly by him and the fear he hadn't wanted her, that he'd been holding back because she'd been somehow damaged or made less fled under the sensual assault.

When he'd strode out to chase off the pizza man, her thoughts scattered at the mouthwatering sight of Brody—all of Brody—save for the towel slung around his hips. She'd never forgotten his exquisite body or how he would lay there and let her explore every curve, every joint, and every muscle. No one was built like him, and if she lived to be a hundred, she couldn't sculpt the perfection she found in his rough-hewn build. Sinew and strength, deadly grace and beauty.

Hitching her thighs around his hips, she let him lead the kiss as he explored her mouth. Vaguely aware of the wall at her back and the hard weight of his erection pressing against her stomach, she feasted on the contact. She could die like this happily drugged from the passion in his kiss. But more than passion and desire, though both lit through her, his kiss held caring. Even holding her, he kept his grip gentle if possessive, and every stroke of his tongue on hers chased away the fear and anxiety of the last several days and left her in a long, slow burn of certainty.

God, she'd missed him. When he finally came up for air, he nuzzled the corner of her mouth. His breathing sounded as ragged as her own, but the hard set of his jaw had relaxed, and his eyes were dark with a savage need she recognized.

"You've been hurt," he said, care and worry slowing the words.

"So?" She didn't dismiss his concerns, but she could feel the thickened whorl of a scar beneath her fingers. She hadn't missed the puckered flesh along his right biceps or the thin, six-inch-long white line stretching from his abdomen to his side. "You've been in way worse situations with bombs, bullets, and crap. I fell out of a car. Big deal."

His eyebrows rose, and the gorgeous line of his mouth turned down at her description. "I'm a Marine."

"Yeah, well, I've wrestled with said Marine before. I think I can handle it." Where the hell the need to push him came from, she didn't know, but she embraced it. He'd been so careful with her from the moment he'd walked in the door. She didn't want careful, she wanted Brody.

All of him.

A smile softened his expression. "Are you sure? You've had a hell of a last few days." And he couldn't stop protecting her; he didn't have it in his nature. Their first night together, he'd done the exact same thing. Given her everything and taken nothing for himself. If she'd not been willing to try and touch him, he'd never have asked her. Maybe he didn't see it, but she did. He took care of people—*his* people.

He'd taken care of her. Later, he'd reached out to Logan and Zach when Jazz had been hurt. She knew he'd been boots on the ground that day, and though he'd never said the words aloud, she'd heard the worry for his friends in his voice. Again and again, whether it was Marines he sent home in hospital choppers or body bags, every single one had left a mark on him. Her heart may never recover from hearing Rebel's injuries could have been his.

And here he was again, fresh off a plane without a thought for himself or his needs, wanting to take care of her.

"You know? The last few days have sucked." Honesty, he deserved it. "I'm not pretending they haven't. I hate what that man did, I hate that he was in my place, that he shot Katrina, and that he tried to take me. I hate that because of him I'm *here* hiding away, and I hate the fact I get queasy with so many men giving me orders and making decisions and crowding around me...." She tightened her hands on his shoulders.

It wasn't only the fact that the men around her were giving her orders or too close for comfort. No, she suffered from more than her old hang-ups. Katrina had been shot defending her, and every single one of those men outside her door were willing to put themselves in front of a bullet. The man in her arms? Brody would do it without even a shadow of hesitation. And it scared the shit out of her.

"I know, and I'm going to fix all of it." A promise. His promise. Brody brushed a gentle kiss to her forehead, then set her down. All that raw passion, he contained it with an effortlessness she envied. No, damn it, she craved more than his restraint.

"Wait." She followed him when he fell back a step, never losing contact. He peeled her hands off of him then pressed a kiss to the bruises on her wrists. "Brody—"

"It's okay," he told her. "I'm going to get dressed, and then we can eat." He pivoted and headed out of the kitchen.

Unwilling to let it go, and annoyed, she chased after him. One step into the bedroom, he stripped off the towel, and Shannon stared at the taut line of his ass. Like the rest of him, there was nothing spare, just hard, cut muscles rippling with his every step. While his arms and face were darkly tanned, his ass and legs weren't. Combat gear didn't leave much for the sun to touch.

"Would you stop?"

His back stiffened at her words, but he ceased moving away from her. "Shannon." His voice sounded unnaturally thick, as though it took tremendous effort to even say her name. "I'm trying to do the right thing here. You're not ready."

"Who says?" Irritation struck a match in her system.

He angled his head, only enough to seet her. "You did. It's been a hellish last few days, the last thing you need is...."

"Is what? Touching you? Having you touch me?" Where the hell her boldness came from she had no idea, but she went with it. Especially if it meant he would stop walking away from her.

With a sigh, he faced her. "You've got injuries...."

"Really?" Because from where she stood, she could see the wear and tear of his years in the Marines etched into every gorgeous muscle on his body.

"Yes, really." The words were a plea. "Go out and get the pizza. We can eat together. We don't have to do anything else."

They didn't? If his intention was to drive her crazy, he'd already succeeded. Grasping the hem of her shirt, she dragged it up and over her head. Her shoulders and back protested the treatment, but she ignored them. She'd been sore and stiff for two days. Everything hurt.

Everything had hurt until he'd touched her, then she forgot about being in pain or afraid. She'd spent too many years studying the human body to be ashamed of hers. His whole posture froze, and she let the shirt drop to the floor. "Yes, I'm hurt. I have bruises." And she turned so he could see her back. She hadn't seen it, but if it matched on the outside the way it felt on the inside, then it probably was a shock. "My arm is scraped up."

With her back still to him, she stuck her thumbs into the waistband of her pants and shoved them and her panties down at the same time. "I'm pretty sure my ass is bruised, too." Kicking the clothes away, she continued her circuit until she faced him once more. "My boobs hurt. My face hurts. And my soul hurts. But you know what doesn't hurt?"

"What?" One syllable, low, rough, and hard. Her nipples tightened to stiff points under the heavy weight of his gaze.

"You touching me. You kissing me. You." Her courage threatened to flee, but she dared to close the distance between them because he hadn't walked away. "I've missed you."

His hard stance cracked, and his eyes softened. "I missed you, too, and I don't want to push you."

Her. He wanted to take care of her, and she melted on the inside. Brody put her needs above his own. He'd done it from the first day they met; he gave and gave and gave, never asking for anything in return. Hell, he was on his first leave in forever, and he'd come straight to her and seemed ready to take on her problems.

"You're not pushing me," she said in a soft voice. "In fact, you're way over there." Extending her arm to prove a point, she traced her fingers over his chest. His heart had to be going a million miles an hour. Maybe he could discipline every other part of him, but his heart gave him away. Dipping her gaze down to the length of his hard cock, she smiled. Well, one of the two things that gave him away.

"I don't want to hurt you." The reluctance in his tone couldn't be manufactured. She dared to go a little closer, and when she slid her arm around his neck, his arms came around her, caging her in. Shannon rested her head to his chest. He smelled of the same soap she used, clean and masculine. His flesh practically burned her, and the last knots of tension bulging in her spine let go.

"You would *never* hurt me." Maybe he didn't understand

or believe it, but she did. "Please, Brody?"

With a groan, he lifted her, then his mouth found hers, and her world began to spin again. As before, he took control of the kiss, demanding and playful in the same breath. His tongue plunged deep, and she met him stroke for stroke. Somehow, she'd forgotten how wonderful he tasted, but no sooner did his tongue swirl with hers than he moved on. A nuzzle to the corner of her mouth, a nip to her jaw, then a hesitation and the lightest of touches to the scrape on her cheek. He pressed feathery, light kisses to the injury, and she opened her eyes to find him gazing at her with an expression so tender it wrenched her heart.

Drowning in the sensations, she dug her fingers into his shoulders as he settled her on the bed. The blanket was chilly on her back, but Brody followed her down, and the heat rolling off him threatened to burn her up. He trailed kisses along her throat, stopping at her shoulders.

She had another set of bruises there, and he laved his tongue over the sorest point. She tried to hold still for him, but he seemed intent on tasting every inch of her skin. When he reached her breasts, she wasn't prepared for the light scrape of his teeth or the way he latched onto one nipple before moving to the next. Every pull sent another pulse to her sex, and she squirmed.

Brody caught her ass in a firm grip, but instead of squeezing, he held her still, and he went back to the first nipple he'd kissed and sucked hard. A low groan broke free, and she ran her fingers over his scalp. His hair was so short, soft and bristly at the same time. The weight of his erection pressed against her leg, and she tried to shift. She wanted to touch him how he did her, but when she stretched a hand between them, he gave her nipple a bite with just an edge of sting, and she gasped.

Lifting his head, he gazed at her with drowsy dark eyes. "You touch me and I'm going to go off all over your hand. And that's not where I want to come."

The words sent another pulse singing through her nerves, and her sex clenched, already imagining him inside of her. "Then hurry." She wanted to lose herself in his touch and feel him surging in her.

He met her demand with a chuckle and cupped his palm on her sex, one finger gliding between the labia to circle her clit, and she arched her hips up to meet the caress. Tension wound upward, spiraling her tighter as he continued to tease without quite touching.

"Mean," she whispered, then laughed as he eased one finger inside of her. When his finger curled and added pressure on her inner wall, her eyes crossed.

"I forgot how tight you are, sweetheart." His pleasure turned the words into a compliment. He continued to tease her, thrusting his finger in gently and pausing to add more pressure to the stroke. Sweat dampened her forehead, and a fresh wave of arousal skated through her system. "We're going to go slow, even if it kills me."

It would kill them both. She'd never felt so ready for him, and she grimaced, wanting to protest, then he added a second finger to the first while pressing her clit with his thumb, and she forgot how to breathe. The second stroke of his thumb erased her thoughts. He continued to kiss a lazy path across her abdomen, but she always knew when he found a bruise or a scrape. He paused, his hand slowing while he kissed the injury.

So much care went into every touch, and tears filled her eyes when he took a moment to gently nuzzle her hip. The bruise had darkened to a lovely shade of deep purple. "Does it hurt, baby?"

"Not right now." No, nothing hurt. She tumbled along a lazy river of pleasure.

The faint rub of his cheek on her inner thigh gave her the only warning she had before his mouth fastened on her clit. The slow drift became a raging rapid, and she catapulted from one explosive orgasm to the next. Fisting the blankets, she tried to hold back her shout, then he vibrated his tongue and the world splintered. She bucked under his mouth, and he kept her where he wanted. Though she floated down, little sparks sizzling through her system, he continued to nuzzle and lick along the seam of her labia, returning time and again to tease her clit.

Surely he was ready, but no—he seemed utterly content to continue exploring her sex with the same thoroughness he'd applied to her injuries, teasing her to the brink before easing her back again and again. He seemed determined to drag this out, and she twisted slightly, trying to see him. The sight of his dark head moving against her sex was nearly as erotic as the feeling of his tongue thrusting into her. No, he wouldn't be hurried.

As if sensing her thoughts, he glanced up and met her gaze. Something inside her softened further, and her thighs clenched as he swirled his tongue. Nothing mattered when they were together. Nothing. Not her stalker. Not the military. Not all the months and distance that had separated them. The heat in his eyes burned all the rest to ash.

With a kiss to her inner thigh, he lifted his head. "What are you thinking about?"

"You," she admitted with a sigh. It didn't matter that he'd already given her an orgasm, she was still hungry for him. The need to have him zinged through her system, an electric tingle racing along her spine. Could he see what he did to her?

"I want to play with you for hours," he said, dragging a finger through her labia again. "I want to see you come over and over. Do you have any idea how fucking gorgeous you are when you cry out?"

She believed him. "Anything you want." Anything. If he wanted to keep her on the edge for hours, fine. If he wanted to melt her into a puddle of wanton need, she could take it, too. Adoration shone in his hard face.

"Be careful," he teased, but the way he said the two words held as much joy as they did warning. "I'll take everything."

"Yeah?" She didn't believe him. He gave everything, too.

"Oh, yeah." And he licked her from her entrance to her clit and down again, never once looking away. The naked desire in his eyes made her heart skip a beat, and she didn't try to suppress the low throaty cry as he continued to torment her sensitive flesh.

"Yes," she called out as he locked his lips around her clit and sucked it hard against his teeth. The pressure built up to an almost unbearable level, then he backed off again and she shook with both laughter and frustration. "Anything you want."

Anything. Everything. She wanted to give it all to him. Every night she went to bed and hoped she would dream of him—because in her dreams she could wake in his arms, feel his hands on her, and know absolute security with him. If she wanted to play, he would lie still for her and let her explore his body, do whatever she wanted. He was her toy and her canvas—how could she be any less?

"Don't move." He rose so swiftly she wanted to keen from his absence. The world seemed so much colder and lonelier without him.

Obeying him didn't mean she couldn't watch. He walked back into the bathroom, returning seconds later, a foil package in hand. Standing at the foot of the bed, he stared at her. The intensity in his attention seemed to stroke over her even though he didn't touch.

Stretching, she held her hand out to him, beckoning him with a curl of her fingers. "I won't break. I promise."

"You break me."

The confession tightened the fist around her heart.

"Then I'll put you back together again," she promised. "Come with me, Brody."

He ripped the foil and rolled the condom on while she watched. Slowly, too slowly, he slid back onto the bed, his body covering hers as his legs nudged hers apart to create a place for him. Nothing about him was small, and she had no doubts about the strength or his skill. A big, bad, dangerous man and all hers.

The thought sparked a second, and she ran her hands up his chest as he braced himself with one arm on either side of her. "You can be on top," he told her suddenly. The offer pulled her inside out. Always thinking about her, making sure she felt safe, confident, and not afraid.

She shook her head because she didn't have the words to express all the feelings tangling together in her mind. Here—with him—she was home. Connected. "I'm right where I want to be."

"So am I." The words were a benediction. He lined his cock up, then pressed in hard. No teasing, no play—just Brody, pushing his body into hers in one long, continuous thrust. It had been over a year for both of them, and he filled her, stretching her to match him. She wrapped her legs around him, battling her body's aches to meet him, hold him to her.

He didn't stop moving; however, he found a rhythm that seemed as natural as breathing, every stroke bringing him closer to her, and then his mouth caught hers, and he stole her breath. Fisting his hands in her hair, he kept her head where he wanted it and plundered, his tongue matching his cock's thrusting motion.

Pinned by his delicious weight, she fought to pull him even closer, and still he didn't stop kissing her—or maybe it was she who couldn't stop tasting him. She couldn't get enough, couldn't stand any distance. Her breasts were crushed to his chest, and every glide of their movement sent wave upon wave of delicious friction. Twisting his hips, he caught her leg and lifted it higher, then he went deep, every thrust catching her clit and deeper still, as though he were pounding himself into her very pores.

Maybe he was, and she held on as the tension in her coiled so tightly, a spring ready to snap, then her orgasm smashed through her. She screamed his name. His shout joined hers, and the glorious tension threaded his body, turning him to solid steel against her until he drove in once more and stilled.

Tangled together, he began to relax, and he nuzzled her mouth gently as his muscles loosened. Settling, he pressed his face to her throat. She floated there, drifting on a current of peace she hadn't experienced in far too long.

"Welcome home," she whispered, and he answered with a gentle kiss. Her Brody was home. Everything would be all right. She could stand anything life threw at her.

She had her Marine.

Chapter Six

$\mathcal{B}$rody returned to the bedroom with the beer and a full box of pizza. Shannon lifted her head from the pillow and stared at him. Humor curved her lips, and her laughter was a balm for the soul.

Pretending an affront, he paused and raised his eyebrows. "Something wrong with the pizza you *ordered*?"

"Midnight snack in bed served by a gorgeous man?" She dragged herself up to a sitting position, absolutely unabashed by her own nudity. "Not a damn thing."

Soft, tousled and smiling was how she should always look. Chuckling, he set the pizza box on the bed and the beer on the nightstand along with the water bottles. "Do you have a preference?" He motioned to the drinks.

"They gave me sedatives." She pointed to a prescription bottle. "I don't think I should drink and have those, too."

Picking up the bottle, he scrutinized the label. "Have you had any today?"

"No. I took them after they brought me back here the first night. I didn't like how they made me feel." After opening the box, she selected a slice and balanced it with two hands. It wasn't remotely warm anymore, but his mouth watered all the same. With a toss, he sent the bottle of sedatives to land in the trashcan on the far side of the room. The rattle echoed loudly.

"Want a beer now?" He didn't bother to hide his grin at her laugh. In the hours since he'd arrived, her pinched expression had relaxed. She had relaxed.

"Mind if I split yours?" She patted the bed next to her, and he obliged her request.

"Not at all." He popped the cap off the first one and passed it over. Even after sating his initial lust, his body still stirred at the sight of her taking a long drink. "You should get some sleep." Uncertain of the time, he glanced over his shoulder at the digital clock face. Barely twenty hundred. He wanted to call Foster, see what the detective learned. Whoever her attacker was, he'd gone from sending notes to trying to take Shannon in a matter of days. Brody didn't need to be a profiler to recognize the escalation as dangerous and odd.

"I'm not tired— I mean I am. But I'm not sleepy." She picked a slice of pepperoni off the pizza and turned it over, studying it.

The last thing he wanted to do was douse her simple joy with reality, but the clock on how long he had till NCIS came calling continued to tick. "You up for talking about the letters and the kidnapping attempt?"

"Probably wouldn't help us if I said I never wanted to talk about it." She sighed and nibbled another bite. He passed the beer to her to wash it down and waited for her to decide. He didn't have to wait long. "I don't understand it."

"What part?"

"Any of it." She spread her arms. "Brody, look at me. I'm an artist." He had a hard time not looking at her. Gorgeous, curvy, and muscled—the perfect example of the feminine form. Strong and delicate, bold and fragile. "Okay, I didn't mean look at me like *that*."

"Like what?" Because he could stare at her all day. Leaning in, he nibbled the sauce staining the corner of her mouth, and her lips parted to greet his kiss. Soft, like her, edged with enough demand to send a pulse to his cock and wake him up. The combination of beer, pizza, and Shannon was a heady cocktail.

"Like you want to eat me up," she said against his lips.

"Hmm, tempting." But as much as he'd like to keep her in this bed for days, they had work to do. Though keeping her in his bed had its advantages—no one else would get near her.

With reluctance, she settled back on the pillows. "You have to ask your questions."

"Yeah, babe. I do." He drained the last of the first beer and then opened a second. "Before Lauren found those letters, had you received others?"

"I have no idea," she answered immediately, and when he frowned, she continued, "No, I mean it. I don't really go through the mail often."

"What do you do with it?"

"With the orders coming in over the last year, I simply haven't had time." Finished with her slice of pizza, she accepted the bottle and took a long drink, then the second slice he offered her. She definitely needed to eat more. "So, a lot of times, the mail is delivered and it sits in a pile by the front door until I get to it. I haul it upstairs and leave it on the counter. Jeanine or Henry will come by and pick it up. They deal with anything involving business."

The couple acted as her agent and business manager. He'd met them briefly during his leave in Dallas the same week he'd spent with Shannon. They were...remarkably unremarkable. "And they hadn't been by in the weeks leading up to your Boston trip?"

She stretched her leg out, one foot balancing on his calf, and he studied the contrast of her painted delicate toes against his ruddier skin. "You know, they were busy. Jeanine was dealing with the details at the gallery there, and she has other clients. Henry...wait, no. Henry stopped by."

"When?"

Teeth dragging over her lower lip, she shook her head. "I have no idea. Let me think." Fortunately, she took a bite of pizza and chewed it with an air of deliberation. Tipping the bottle back, Brody took a long drink. Chances were the detective had already spoken to her manager and agent. They were deeply involved in helping her career. Hell, Jeanine encouraged her to try the service that introduced Shannon to him in the first place.

"I was working on practice pieces. I'd done sketches, and I needed to make the models to see how well the sketches translated to stone. I half-thought I might try woodcarving, but I am just better with marbles and stones. I'd finished Logan's piece, and I had just started on Matt's. I had problems really capturing Jethro." While she spoke, she mimed the motion of carving with her hand. He had to wonder if she was even aware of her actions. "I finished Matt's piece about four weeks before I went to Boston. His is only the second of the six practice pieces. I didn't do Rebel's until last...." Nose scrunched, she looked adorable.

The Rebel piece was one he'd asked her to do, and he'd sent her photographs Rebel's fiancée had provided. He owed a debt of gratitude to Reb's case nurse—now his fiancée—but visiting her and Rebel would have to wait.

"So, you're saying roughly four weeks before you left for Boston. You were in Boston around two weeks, and you've been home nearly a week. So, around seven weeks or so since the last time your mail was picked up."

"Wow. I suck." Her eyes rounded, and she grimaced before taking the beer out of his hand and drinking.

Chuckling, he waited for her to finish her drink before passing her another slice. "You don't suck." Eating two slices in rapid succession, Brody considered what she'd told him. She could have received the letters for weeks. The escalation may not have been sudden. Maybe, instead, it had been a direct retaliation for her failure to act on whatever the writer had wanted her to do. "Tell me about the hotel break-in."

Wiping her fingers on a napkin, she repeated the details from the moment she and Liam had left the elevator to when security arrived, including how she'd fallen inside and hit her head and the man catching her shoulder with his foot before he grappled with Liam. "But I think he was more interested in getting away than in hurting me."

Maybe. And if she'd been alone when she'd returned to her hotel room? If Liam hadn't insisted on accompanying her to her door? "Did Liam take you to your room every night?"

"No, actually, I had been giving him a hard time for insisting the night of the gallery opening, but I was really tired, too. He's a good friend, he had to rescue me from three conversations where the people were pretty pushy, and I know I was swaying on my feet after all was said and done."

"Your normal pattern included driving back to the hotel and going up alone?" So, Liam's presence could have thrown a wrench in the person's plans. Making Boston the first attempt, which would explain the preparation for hitting her loft in Dallas. If he'd already been interrupted once, he wouldn't have wanted a second problem.

"Brody?"

"Yeah, babe?"

"I don't understand why anyone would do this to me. Lauren said she had her dealings with stalkers. That makes sense. She's an actress. People saw her in movies and on television. Nobody sees me. I'm in my workshop ninety percent of the time."

"But *Her Marine* made a name for you. It's been a big hit, right?" She'd sent him some clippings from a couple of magazines and the paper. "You raised money with the showings. Luke mentioned you'd done a donation, too."

Cheeks flushing pink, Shannon nodded. "But those were always about the piece. Not me...." She looked at her hands, which she'd begun to twist together.

"What?" He nudged her gently.

"One interviewer wanted to know my inspiration, and I talked about you. A lot." With a wince, she stole a glance at him, and her blush deepened.

Brody smiled. "I have no problems with you talking about

me."

"Well, I may have gone on at length about how noble and brave and handsome and sweet you are." Shyness rippled through her expression, and she laughed. Pride fisted in his chest, and he caught her chin with a finger and nudged her gaze back up again.

"Thank you," he said. No way she could understand what her adoration meant to him or that she thought of him at all. "Do you want to know something utterly unrelated to any of this?"

"Yes," she said with a nod then caught his hand in hers. He liked the way her hands felt. They were scraped at the moment, nails split and a little rough from working with her stone. But they were also soft and feminine, as gentle in their strength as she was.

"For the last fifteen years, the Marines were my family. My only family. I signed up the day after my eighteenth birthday. If I hadn't needed my high school diploma, I would have hitchhiked my way to the boot. Sergeant Messer knew it, too. He was the recruiter I met during career week. Tough son of a bitch. Hard as nails and had no tolerance for attitude, but if you asked him for questions or help? He was right there. He knew my situation, met my foster folks, and sat me down and said, 'Finish school, get your diploma, play it straight, and then you go Marine, and you go hard.'" Damn, he hadn't thought of Messer in years. "He promised to have my back, and he did. It was a shit three months between the day I signed up and the day I walked across the stage with my diploma. Messer sat right there in the audience. He took me out for dinner afterward, and the next day, he drove me to the airport and put me on a plane."

"He sounds wonderful." She tightened her grip on his hand, and Brody tried to relax his fingers. His knuckles had gone white.

"Yeah, well, not sure he'd like that description. But he was there when I graduated boot. Slapped me on the shoulder and then congratulated me because I'd qualified for OCS—Officer Candidate School. Said he expected the next time he saw me, he'd be saluting me." Lifting their joined hands, he brushed a kiss to her knuckles. She really had done a number on them. Closing the pizza box, he set it aside then pulled her over into his lap.

Cuddling with Shannon had to be the best part of being home. No matter how brief his sojourn would be, he planned to touch her often. "My point is," he said as she settled her head on his shoulder. "Messer was the only guy on my side, and then I graduated OCS and received my first orders. I met Luke and, later, Logan and Damon. Zach, too. Those guys are family. Matt came into the unit later, so did James. But Messer was first. I watched a lot of the guys around us have to say goodbye to their families, their loved ones when we shipped out. Never had anyone out there been waiting for me. Sometimes I think it was easier. Luke had his dad in the Corps. He was over there in the thick of it with us, but you know he left a girl."

God, he rambled. A couple of beers made him maudlin. There was a reason he didn't drink much.

"Anyway, I didn't have someone to come home to...until you. The last couple of years, you've been my compass. My true north. You were home. So, thank you." Damn it sounded lame. He'd never been good at the mushy crap.

She shifted in his lap, wiggling around until she straddled his legs, and damn, it turned him on to have her moving all around him, but the gentleness in her face arrested the teasing remark on his tongue. "What happened to Messer?"

Crap, she'd caught that. "He died in the first Iraq offensive, before we took Baghdad."

"I'm so sorry." She cradled his face, and fresh tears glimmered in her eyes.

"Me, too." Messer hadn't been the first, and God knew he wouldn't the last. "I had the guys by then, so I wasn't alone."

"But you feel every death," she said. He'd never said aloud, hell, he didn't even tell the shrinks when he had to get his psych evals. They didn't want to worry he might snap.

"That's the cost of living." Running his fingers through her hair, he let the strands fall through his fingers. "You're the prize."

"Oh?" Her eyebrows rose. "I didn't realize I was in a cereal box."

Tugging her closer, he grinned. "You're my prize. Cause I sure as hell don't deserve you."

Shannon leaned in and bit his lip, the sting serving only to heat his blood. "I'm the one who doesn't deserve you if we're going to start comparing."

"Hmm." Fisting some of her hair, he urged her closer. "How about we agree to disagree and keep each other anyway?"

A breathless laugh and a soft kiss were her answer.

"Seriously?" Shannon couldn't be sure she'd heard him right. A part of her regretted the arrival of dawn. All night, they'd played, cuddled, had sex, and even slept. At sunrise, however, Brody had rolled out of bed and done a series of calisthenics that had her thinking about dragging him back to the sheets.

"Yes." He sat on the sofa, lacing up his shoes. Even the sweatpants and T-shirt didn't diminish his masculine presence. "I need a run, and it's a good way to clear your head."

She wore shorts and a tank top and perched on the sofa next to him. "My head is pretty clear."

"Good. We're going to clear my head, and you're not going to be out of my sight." A point he'd driven earlier when he joined her in the shower. The pleasant memory evoked a shudder, and she grinned.

After tying the first shoe, she glanced at him. "You're amazing."

"It's still early, but I'll go with that. Get a move on, Fabray. We've got a five mile loop to do."

"Five miles?" She coughed. Running was one thing but....

"I like to do ten, but five will have to suffice. Need me to make it two for you?" The dare in his eyes lit her up. He could go from sober and serious to playful in a split second.

"No, I can handle five." But she rolled her eyes and finished putting on her second shoe. "I would prefer coffee and a bagel."

"We can have those after. Stretch and warm those muscles up," he ordered and disappeared into the kitchen, returning a moment later with a pair of water bottles. Using a belt, he secured the bottles to his waist.

With a groan, she stood and began to stretch. Amazingly, she felt loose already despite expecting to be sore and tight. Even her bruises felt better today. Arms folded, Brody watched without an ounce of criticism in his expression.

"Hamstrings, too. How's your hip?"

Twisting slowly from side to side, she tested the bruises. The skin pulled taut and ached. "Sore, but I've done worse after finishing a sculpture." Hell, she'd done worse working on the practice pieces. Sometimes when she worked, she had to bend or twist at awkward angles and hold it for hours. Thankfully, she did yoga.

"Good. If it gets worse or you start to really hurt, you tell me." It wasn't a request.

The corner of her mouth curved. "Sir, yes, sir."

"Brat." But he laughed and shook his head when he said it. Only after ten minutes more of stretching did Brody seem satisfied. He'd tucked a phone into his pocket and sent her to grab hers. Outside, he led the way down the stairs. The cool, spring mornings were a distant memory. Already heavy and warm, the day promised to be a typical Texas broiler—though the gray clouds suggested rain.

They probably wouldn't get so lucky.

Shannon had finished pulling her hair back into a ponytail by the time they achieved the ground floor.

"The trail starts there." He pointed to it. "It winds through the property, in and out of the trees, and goes nowhere near the road. It's about two and a half miles, if I recall correctly. There are other routes we can veer off on, but there are markers for every tenth of a mile, so we can keep track. If you need to slow down, we slow down. If we have to walk part of it, we walk."

"And when we pass out from heat exhaustion?" She wanted to take the words back the minute she'd said them, but he laughed at her and gave her ponytail a gentle tug.

"I've been in your studio when you're working. Jungles are cooler. You're not going to pass out." Another reason she adored him, he didn't treat her like she was weak. With him, she always felt stronger.

"You have a point. Can we go back there today?" Not that she didn't appreciate the way everyone took care of her, but she wanted her space back. Her work.

"I called Detective Foster a little while ago." News to her. "He's going to meet us at your place at ten and take me through the scene and go over what he has so far."

The scene. Damn it, she'd forgotten it was technically a crime scene. She should call Katrina today. "Okay."

"Shannon?" The deep timbre of his voice pulled her back to the present. "You stay right next to me on the trail. You set the pace, and I'll match it."

"I'm going to be slower than you normally would run." She held no illusions about the comparison of their physical fitness.

"Right next to me," he repeated.

"Sir, yes, sir." And instead of pacing away, he leaned over and pressed a kiss to her lips.

"You need to say that when we're in bed." A dark thrill raced through her system. "In fact, I think I'm going to order you to say it in bed."

"Sir," she replied, drawing out the words. "Yes, sir."

His slow grin had her heart twisting. Everything about him was beautiful. She wanted more hours with him, more than stolen moments enjoyed on leave. No, she wanted years.

"Anytime now, babe." He gave her a nudge, waiting for her to get moving.

Biting back another sir, yes, sir, she rolled her shoulders and set off at an easy jog. Better to warm up the rest of her. Brody fell in beside her like they did this every day—the most natural thing in the world. Beside her.

Yeah, she wanted that.

By the half-mile mark, she'd warmed up and increased her pace. They ran side-by-side, the slap of their shoes against the pavement in sync. Laughter bubbled through her at the first mile marker. The shadow of the last forty-eight hours finally slid off of her.

"For someone who doesn't like to run, you're not bad," Brody said, and unlike her, he wasn't even panting.

"Just because I don't like something, doesn't mean I don't know how to do it." Confession time. "I ran in high school and then later in college. I stopped for a long time. Almost forgot how much I used to enjoy it." The surge of endorphins when she pushed her body, the strength and the speed—the freedom. He didn't ask her why she stopped. After the rape, she'd retreated from whole swaths of her life. Not intentionally, but somehow she'd managed to do it anyway.

"You're doing good, keep your chin up. Looking down throws off your form." The suggestion, like so much else he did, wrapped around her like an embrace. Always watching out for her.

"Yes, sir." Buoyed by the simple joy, she let out another laugh as they hit the two-mile mark. The landscape around them was beautiful, thick and green. It was still early enough in summer for the heat not to have burned the trees to an early yellow or fried the grass. Fresh cut grass and cedar mulch perfumed the moist air.

"When did you start running again?" He saved the question until they cruised past the building housing her borrowed apartment. Others were waking, and she caught sight of another man hitting the trail ahead of them. He waved to Brody but didn't slow his pace or drop back to join them.

"About eighteen months ago, right around the time I signed up for a self defense class." His jerk told her she'd surprised him. "I know, I didn't tell you." She had to slow some by the third mile. Running and talking was harder than she thought. "I wanted it to be a surprise."

"What kind of self-defense?"

"Basic stuff...kind of street fighting but with the goal of getting away." Not that it had done her a damn bit of good when that bastard grabbed her. Panic hadn't been her friend. "I volunteer at a Jewish community center, teach art to some of the kids a couple of times a month. Zehava—she runs the place—held some classes for women in the neighborhood."

A stitch in her side added to her discomfort, but she pushed past it and kept running. The last couple of miles still stretched out in front of them. "Anyway," she panted. "Fighting takes a lot of air, apparently. The instructor suggested we amp up our cardio, and since I didn't do any, I remembered running and went out for a jog. The first one...yeah, that sucked. I made it two blocks and wheezed like a forty-year-old smoker. But I also felt good. So, I started doing it more regularly."

"You run outside? In your neighborhood?" Thunder rumbled in his tone. And damn, he still didn't sound like he found it hard to talk.

"Three days a week, or at least I try. Sometimes I get caught up and don't get out to run. But I've been trying. It's liberating. So is knowing how to kick a man in the groin and gouge out his eyes." With a grimace, she slowed her pace again. The cramp in her side really hurt.

"Walk." Brody caught her arm and slowed her when she would have kept going. She dropped out of the run, and her muscles were all protesting from her calves to her quadriceps. The burn had her sweating, and she could feel the tautness threatening to cramp, so she kept walking and gulped air gratefully. "I told you to tell me when it hurt."

"It's the talking with the running." She tried to make an excuse, but one sideways look at him and she knew he wasn't buying it. "You're right. I'm sorry. I wanted to show off and do the whole five with you."

"Hmm," was his only comment. "So, self-defense classes and you run regularly in your neighborhood."

"Yeah, I thought it would be good to know, give me more confidence about getting out of my comfort zone." Considering how narrow the zone actually was, she wanted to be stronger. Better for Brody, if she were to be completely honest, but considering the scowl he wore, she decided it best not to mention that at the moment. "It worked. When I went to Boston the first time, I was scared, but I-I don't know how to describe it. I knew I could do it, fear or no fear."

He passed her a bottle of water wordlessly.

Twisting to walk sideways, she studied him. "You're not mad, are you?"

"No," he responded quickly and gave her a tight smile. "But you running regularly, that's not a usual habit of yours. It's another change...."

Oh. A shiver raced up her spine. "You think he's been watching me."

"Yeah, babe. I do." They were at the four-mile mark when he opened his water bottle and drained it. She would have started to run again, but he shook his head. "You're limping."

Only a slight limp, but she felt the ache of the run all through her left leg, and the bruise on her hip pulsed like she could feel the blood rushing to it. "Not badly."

"Good, let's keep it not badly." With his hand still on her arm, he shifted them to the right side of the path, with her on the inside and him on the outside, to let other runners pass.

"You notice *everything*." Noticed and responded to it, too. Whether they were in the shower or sitting on the bed eating pizza.

"Training." He shrugged. "Be aware. Be responsible. Be

safe."

"Can I ask you about being over there?" Should she ask? Did he want to talk about his service?

"Do you want to know?" No judgment twisted in the question, and made it easier to answer.

"I want to know everything about you. But I don't want you to hurt. If you don't want to talk about it, don't. If you do, then I'm all ears."

He gave her a sidelong look and a half-smile. "I think your ears are sexy, but I like the rest of you, too."

Now, she rolled her eyes and gave him a light tap on the arm. "You know what I meant."

Approval softened his expression. "Yes, I do. And I'll answer anything you want to ask me. It was a job in a hellhole, sweetheart. Nothing pretty or sweet-smelling about it. Most of my jobs are in hellholes. You get used to it."

"I hate that you have to get used to anything along those lines." She'd have to have been living under a rock to not be aware of the various hot spots he'd served in. Knowing and understanding didn't go hand-in-hand. Her exile and isolation were self-imposed, but she could still go to the corner and get an expensive coffee or drive to a mall and shop. She had air conditioning and heat—access to food delivery. Really, her hardships were no comparison.

"You forget, I volunteered." He slowed his pace again, they were nearing the end of the five miles and her legs were on fire, but she'd kept up—mostly. "I had a job to do, and I did it."

Biting her lip, she fought to find the courage to ask the question she really wanted to know the answer to. "Are you going to go back?"

"I may not have a choice, sweetheart." Another shrug, but his expression shut down and closed her out. "We'll tackle that when we need to, okay?"

"Okay."

The companionable silence lasted till the apartment building was in sight. Luke Dexter headed in their direction, his pace and manner suggesting they were his targets, and Brody stiffened next to her.

"Everything all right?" The captain was his best friend. Shouldn't he be happier to see him?

"It's fine." For the first time, she heard the lie in his tone. With a smile, he glanced at her. "I'll walk you up to the apartment, and you can shower while I talk to Luke."

Yes, she definitely needed another shower, but uneasiness slid through her. When they reached Luke, the two men nodded and Brody told him the same thing. "Give me a minute. I want to get Shannon inside."

They didn't shake hands or greet each other in any way two friends should have. Luke followed them up the stairs, which meant she couldn't ask. At the door, Brody opened the apartment. "Wait with Luke a second." Then he headed inside.

Of course, he would check it before he let her go in. A moment later, he returned.

"You're good. Go shower." He gave her a light nudge. "I'll be right with you."

She wanted to argue with him. His expression remained tight, and Luke's stony silence practically shouted something else was going on, but Brody held the door open for her and waited.

"You'll tell me if something is wrong, right?" She couldn't leave it alone.

"If you need to know, I will," he said and, though not a real answer, she couldn't ignore the quiet urging in his eyes. Acquiescing, she gave Luke a small smile and brushed her hand to Brody's chest. Whatever was going on, he wanted to talk to his friend alone. She could give him that much.

The door closed behind her, but if the men said anything, she couldn't hear them. For a split second, she was tempted to lean her head on the door and listen, and then shame flushed through her. Spying on Brody suggested she didn't trust him.

No, she wouldn't disrespect him in such a way. Trusting him was easy, so she held onto the feeling and marched back to the bedroom they'd shared the night before. In the shower, she tipped her face up to the water and sighed.

If nothing else, the run had proved her alive and capable. Between that and Brody, her week definitely had taken a turn for the better.

Still...whatever he and Luke needed to talk about, she hoped for no more bad news.

Chapter Seven

*L*uke rounded on Brody seconds after he closed the door and locked Shannon inside. "What the hell were you thinking?" Fortunately, he kept his voice pitched low and quiet. They knew how to talk and not let it carry.

He didn't pretend to misunderstand. "You didn't need to know."

"Yes, I did."

"No." Brody shook his head. "What you don't know you can't be charged with, and it can't blow back on you." He wasn't an idiot. Mike's Place had a lot of private funds, but it also had generous government grants and support from those in uniform. The last thing Luke needed was to be associated with Brody's illegal choice.

"Lieutenant, don't be an ass. You're still one of *my* men whether you report to me or not. You didn't think this through." In leveling the charge, Luke was absolutely correct.

"She needed me." Brody wouldn't apologize or make an excuse for it. "When she's secure, I'll report in."

Sighing, Luke leaned against the railing and looked thoughtful. Civilian life agreed with him. He'd let his hair grow out and he appeared less careworn than in his last tour. Maybe marriage, not civilian life, did it for him.

"I'm sorry I put you in this position," Brody said. His

former captain deserved that much at least. "And thank you for taking care of her."

"Yeah, she's yours, so that makes her ours, but if I'd known you were going to pull this crap, I'd never have called you." An empty threat.

"Bullshit."

Luke laughed, but it had very little humor. "You need to get off property today. There's an inspection coming through, two generals and one colonel. They'll have aides with them."

Nodding once, Brody met his gaze. "Understood. I'll rent a car."

"No need." He held out a set of keys. "Logan and Zach picked up Shannon's car when we brought her to the property. We've been over it. No unpleasant surprises waiting. When you get to the vehicle, you might find a couple of burner phones in the front seat and some supplies—and some walking-around money."

"You could get in a hell of a lot of trouble...."

"For giving you keys?" The man may have retired, but he'd lost none of his edge. "I doubt it. Don't get stupid. And take care of your girl." Pivoting on his heels, Luke headed for the stairs, but paused a few steps away. Without turning, he said, "Give me a heads up when you're good to go. I've still got friends. We'll see you through this."

No way in hell would he ask Luke to go out on a limb for him.

"That's an order, Marine."

Brody smiled faintly. "Sir, yes, sir."

The man disappeared down the steps and left Brody holding her keys. Yeah, the men in his unit were family. If he needed them, he had no doubts about whether they would be there.

Pocketing the keys, he pulled out his phone and memorized the detective's information before shutting it off. In the kitchen, he opened the phone and stripped out the battery. Doing so probably blew the warranty, but better than having them activate it remotely. He hid the phone debris in his bag before detouring to the bathroom. Shannon stood in front of the sink, wrapped only in a towel.

His cock twitched, almost hopeful, and he sighed. Yeah, he'd love to strip the towel off and play for a while, but they had work to do.

"Is everything all right?"

Meeting her questioning gaze in the mirror, he gave her a small smile and paused to kiss bare shoulder. "It will be." Not a lie, and he meant it. "You did great on the run."

"Pfft, I didn't even make it that far past mile three. I held you back." Still, her face lit up at his compliment.

"Can't hold a man back when he's where he wants to be." He stripped out of his clothes and reached over to turn the shower on. Shannon's gaze stroked over him like a caress, and he resisted the urge to puff out his chest. The fact she liked looking at him did wonders for his ego. "Behave," he told her sternly. "We have to get dressed, grab you car and some food, and then head back to your place."

Excitement thrummed through her, but he kept an eye on her as he stood under the spray. As swiftly as her joy at being able to go home appeared, it vanished. "Brody...what if he comes back?"

Fine with Brody. He wanted the son of a bitch to show up while he was there. Life would be much simpler, but it would only scare her. "I'll take care of you."

His girl didn't bite, however. She pivoted, hands on her hips, to face him in the shower. "He had a gun."

"Having a gun and keeping a gun are two different things." Brody let the sweat sluice away. Soaping up thoroughly, he rinsed off and glanced toward her. She remained silent. "What?"

"Confidence is sexy, you know." She chewed her on her lower lip and then let the towel drop. "Really, sexy."

With a groan, he shut off the water and stepped out of the shower. "We're going to be late." That didn't stop him from picking her up or her from wrapping her legs around his hips. Ignoring the water dripping off of him and soaking her, he carried her to the bed.

"I can totally skip the bagels," she said before her mouth closed over his and Brody twisted, falling onto the bed and ensuring he landed on bottom. Skipping the bagels definitely worked for him.

It was after nine before he carried their bags to her car—a basic, four-door Toyota Corolla. Her surprise at finding it in the parking lot drew another smile from him. As promised, the phones were in the front seat along with a small case. He put their bags in the trunk and added the cash to his. Luke had left him almost five thousand dollars.

Yeah, he owed the captain.

"I can't believe they thought to get it for me." Hesitation filled her expression, and she studied the sprawling buildings. "I feel like I should tell them I'm sorry for being so...freaked out when they were simply being kind."

"They understand," he said. They had the same training as he did to recognize the symptoms, and most specialized in treating wounded bodies and souls. Her damaged heart meant they took extra care.

Nudging her in the direction of the passenger seat, he held the door open until she seated herself in the car. "This has been a really insane week."

"It's going to get better." No matter what it took, he'd make sure of it. "We need to go. Detective Foster will be at your place at ten."

She made a face, but Brody waited until he'd circled the car and climbed in the driver's seat to question it. "What?"

"It's nothing," She waved it off, but the tapping of her fingers on one thigh and the bounce of her other foot were nervous ticks.

Scanning the area around them, he noted their surroundings and the people in them before starting the car and backing it out of the parking spot. "What, Shannon?"

"He doesn't like me...and I'm pretty sure he doesn't believe me."

For clarity's sake, he asked, "Detective Foster?"

She nodded once and fidgeted. "I think he thinks I'm making this up for some kind of publicity stunt."

That would be the dick approach to take, and Foster hadn't sounded like an asshole on the phone at all. "Why do you think so?" One benefit to their delayed start meant lighter traffic on 75. Well, second benefit. The first had been having Shannon again.

"Because I think it." The words rode out of her in a stampede. She clenched her hands and leaned her head back. "Brody? I'm a *nobody*. Yes, I'm making a name for myself with people who patronize the arts. The work is getting noticed. *Her Marine* got picked for a lot of human interest articles. Fans of it remember the *piece*, not me. I live in the real world. I'm a sculptor. I do commissions, and I create art. But I'm not someone who gets a crazy fan hunting them unless I want my name in the paper and to get some kind of notoriety."

Not an implausible argument, except.... "Did you do all this to get your name in the paper?"

"Of course not!" Frustration ripped through her voice like razor wire. "But why else it would be happening?"

She didn't see why anyone would value her for her, so he attacked from a lateral standpoint. "So, you didn't do this to get your name in the paper. Would Henry or Jeanine?" The couple managed her career and served as an agent to get her work out there. They were the frontline to get to Shannon from a professional standpoint.

"No," she said with a frown of horror. Twisting sideways in the seat, she stared at him. "They're my *friends*."

"Convince me." He switched lanes to pass the truck.

Confusion filtered through her outrage. "What?"

"Convince me. If you think this is the perfect way to get your name in a paper, who benefits?"

"Brody—"

"No," he said and held up his hand. "You get your name in a paper and some notoriety. Who benefits?"

"Well, if I'm not dead, then me." She cleared her throat.

"What about Henry and Jeanine? They still earn money off your work."

"No," she said with a quick shake of her head. "They might get their commissions. But once the work is gone, they wouldn't get anything."

"You have about as much family as I do." He frowned. "You told me they had power of attorney in the event something happened to you." The topic came up during an odd conversation one long evening in Florence, brought on by his increasing need to protect her. "They manage your finances, ensure most of your bills are paid, help negotiate your contracts, and they get a percentage of your success."

"Yes, but they don't have power of attorney anymore." With an impatient shift, she went back to drumming her nails on her thigh.

Brody reached over and caught her hand. "What aren't you telling me?"

"I gave you my power of attorney—in the event of anything medical or...or if I died. You get it. They don't."

The news punched him in the gut, and he relaxed his foot on the accelerator. "When the hell did you do that?" It came out far harsher than he'd intended, and she flinched. "I've been in a war zone more often than not, why would you give it to me?" The moment he asked the question, he realized the answer. A connection. She'd wanted a tangible tie to him, even if it were as intangible as a piece of legal paperwork. "Shannon."

She tried to tug her hand away, but he held it. "I wanted...I wanted there to be a reason for you to come home. If you had to make the decisions, maybe they would have to bring you back. It's stupid, and I know it doesn't work that way, but...."

Lifting her hand to his lips, he brushed a kiss to her

knuckles, and she fell silent. "You didn't want to be alone." But more…. "You didn't want me to feel alone."

Face flushing, she glanced down. "Except you didn't know about it…and you wouldn't have found out unless something bad happened to me."

Something bad had happened to her, but she needed to know she wasn't alone in this choice. "You're listed as my next of kin." He'd also added her name to his accounts, allowing her to collect on his savings in the event anything happened to him. The news startled her, and she jerked. Smiling, he kept her hand hostage and stroked his thumb along the callous at the heel of her palm. "Maybe I needed a tie, too."

With a wobbly, watery laugh she said, "We're a little messed up."

"Nah." He shook his head, and as much as he wanted to pursue this part of the discussion, it would have to wait. "Still, it does eliminate Henry and Jeanine from benefiting if something happens to you."

"So, I convinced you?"

Yes, she had. "Yes, unfortunately."

"Why unfortunately?"

"Because now we need to dig into your life and see if there is anyone else." Or if it really was some crazy fuckwad who'd decided to fixate on her. Zealots were the worst kind of enemy—unpredictable and violent—and the kind likely to strike whenever it pleased them.

"Don't you think I've tried to figure out who it could be?"

"I know you have, but you're too close to the situation." And too nice. "So let's start with old boyfriends."

"I haven't had a boyfriend since high school."

Saying nothing, he merely raised his brows. What did that make him?

"You know what I mean." She banged her head against the seat. "Boyfriend is a label. It means dates and gifts and you know…stuff."

"Uh-huh."

Irritation replaced her earlier embarrassment. "You're my *lover*, Brody. Not my boyfriend."

"As long as you know you're taken, I don't care what label you put on it." Satisfied she didn't dwell on her fear, he grinned. She tugged her hand from his then slapped his shoulder.

"You're mean." The words lacked any real heat, especially when coupled with her giggle.

"I dunno, seems fair that to be your boyfriend I should ask."

"Ask what?"

"Wanna go steady?"

"Promise to carry my books for me?" Her smile lit him up.

"Anywhere you want them to go."

The teasing buoyed her mood, and she was still laughing when he parked in her garage. One nice thing about owning the converted warehouse studio, she had private parking and the automatic door. The problem with it was the time delay between opening, parking, and closing it again. The blind spots created by the vehicle, coupled with distraction, meant anyone could slip in if she didn't pay attention.

"You stay right with me," he told her before getting out of the car. "In my line of sight and within arm's reach."

"I promise." Nothing playful or light marked her response—not even a teasing, sir, yes, sir. Her earlier limp was slightly more pronounced after the car ride. Bruises had a tendency to stiffen, and hers were still in the ugly, dark-colored stage. He left their bags in the car for now and walked with her through a second door to the empty first floor of the warehouse in time to hear the knock on the front door.

Brody checked his watch. One minute to ten. Detective Foster was prompt. The impeccable timing also distracted Shannon from the dark stain on the concrete and the debris left over from the paramedics. No one had cleaned up the crime scene.

Keeping Shannon next to him, he swept a glance over the empty area. It had far too many shadows amidst the pools of muted sunlight filtered through dirty windows. A check through the peephole revealed a man in a pair of slacks, dress shirt, and suit jacket that had all seen better days.

"Describe Foster to me."

She'd stayed with him, and a half step behind exactly as he'd asked. "Mid-thirties. Dirty blond hair, almost brown. Green eyes. Firm mouth, lower lip slightly larger than his upper, white scar cutting the upper lip on the right side about halfway between the midline and the corner of his mouth. Crescent-shaped scar on his right cheekbone, a couple of centimeters below his eye. Oval-shaped jaw, high brow line, eyes a little asymmetrical, and at least two notches in his nose."

Since the man outside resembled her description exactly, Brody opened the door. "Detective."

"Lieutenant." Foster held up his badge, but Brody gave it a cursory inspection and nodded. Withdrawing a step, Brody let the detective inside and studied the cop, well aware he received similar scrutiny in return. "Last time I checked, you were supposed to be in Afghanistan, Lieutenant Essex."

"He's been due home on leave for a while," Shannon answered as she placed her hand on his biceps. She'd moved closer to him. Foster, she'd said earlier, didn't like her much. Maybe what she'd meant is she didn't like him—or perhaps she was simply uncomfortable. "I'm lucky he was able to come home now."

"Maybe too lucky. Mind telling me where you were three nights ago, Lieutenant?"

Shannon bristled at the implication. "Brody is not the one who—"

"Shh." He caught her hand in his and gave it a gentle squeeze but didn't take his gaze off the detective. "It's a fair question, and he's doing his job." But if he didn't back it down a step, Brody might get brought up on charges of assault. He appreciated hardass with the best of them, but not at her expense. "I was in Afghanistan. You can check with my CO or any of my men. You can also check arrivals at DFW yesterday morning. That's when I landed."

Foster nodded once, but his jaw tightened a fraction. The detective looked at Shannon briefly and then back to Brody, but whatever thoughts he considered, he kept them off his face. "All right. You asked me to walk you through what we knew. So here I am. Miss Fabray, you don't have to listen if you're going to be uncomfortable."

The consideration raised Brody's estimation of the man, but it wasn't open for debate. "She doesn't leave my sight."

"And going over it again might jar my memory," Shannon admitted. They hadn't discussed that aspect in the car. His woman was smart and brave.

"All right. Let's go over the night of the attempted kidnapping," Foster took the lead and pointed to the steel door. "Our perp did not enter here, though he did exit. There's a secondary egress located in the back of the building that should have been sealed. It had new hinges, and the old boards had been removed."

Brody went cold. The work had taken forethought and planning. Foster led them to the door.

"Far as we can tell, the work could have been done any time in the last few months. There's no alarm system hooked up to this door, and no cameras facing the alley. According to statements we took from your manager and agent, you don't use this level other than to enter at the front and take the elevator up." He glanced at Shannon for confirmation.

"I don't. I have plans for it eventually, but...." She shrugged. "That's later."

"Right. So, this door had been replaced, and it's got a locking mechanism. Easy enough for the perp to enter and exit through here without anyone knowing." The door in question currently had a crossbar on it. "We've sealed it for now, and techs took finger prints. They found a couple of smudged prints, so they may or may not provide us with some answers. Now, when I talked to Morgan, he and Bates found this door on their initial inspection, but it was secured. Both assumed you had a key." Again, he deferred to Shannon for confirmation.

"No one asked me." The knowledge troubled her, and she worried her lower lip while she stared at the door. "Does this mean whoever this guy is, he's been able to come and go?"

"Yes." Foster didn't blunt the informational blow. "But we suspected as much because the letters were hand delivered. They had no stamps or mailing codes on them. But we're going to come back to that."

So whoever kept coming after her had access at any point? Brody scowled, but stayed focused on the intel.

Foster led them back toward the side stairs and elevator. "Two nights ago, a thunderstorm rolled in. Pretty typical storm."

"It knocked the power out." Shannon rubbed her opposite arm, as if cold.

"No, it didn't." Foster pulled out a penlight and shone it on the fuse box. "He turned the power off."

"He was already inside when Katrina came downstairs." Her jaw tightened, but anger, not fear, flashed in her eyes.

"Exactly. He had to know she was here, he shut it off, and waited for her." Shifting to the side, Foster took a position across from the stairwell. Miming a gun motion with his right hand, he pointed it toward the open door leading up to Shannon's loft. "He waited right here. When she came down...pop. You didn't hear a gunshot?"

"No." Shannon shook her head. "But I'd just gotten out of the shower on the opposite side of the loft from the stairs." Good girl, she was thinking, not just reacting. "The storm was really loud...even the rain beating on the roof is really loud here, not to mention the thunder and the lightning. I don't remember hearing anything sounding like a gunshot."

"So, let's assume he had a silencer. He took out Katrina as

soon as she reached the last step." Foster used the penlight to show them the floor. Darker stains discolored the raw cement. "He waited here until you came to check on her."

"What if I hadn't?"

"You were coming down, babe," Brody answered before Foster could. "You knew she'd headed down here, and then the lights didn't come back on. You were going to check on her. It wasn't a matter of if, only when."

This guy had planned. Brody studied the layout of the empty first floor—wide open, with only the support columns providing any kind of cover. A scattering of overhead lights would give the deeper dark a dingy kind of illumination, but at night, during a storm with the power out?

The perfect trap.

Especially with Katrina's presence offering Shannon the illusion of safety. Gripping her upper arm, he drew her closer to him. Her wobbly smile flashed gratitude in his direction. The patience of this stalker, the details—they suggested a long-term kind of interest. Something had escalated him, but no flash in the pan. He'd been on a slow burn.

"You still good?" The detective's attention remained on Shannon. Because Foster took the time to ask earned him another point in Brody's estimation.

"Creeped out, but I'm okay." She leaned into Brody, and he got what she didn't say. She felt safer because of his presence. Precisely why he'd come.

"You came down the stairs here," Foster pointed. "You up for walking us through the rest?"

Despite his laid back manner, Foster proved capable. His attention didn't waver from Shannon, but he didn't stare. By passing the decision of whether she would repeat what happened to her, he reduced the pressure. Slow and halting at first, Shannon repeated the sequence of events with only the hitches of her breath revealing the fear, but when she described the trip to the car, Foster frowned.

"After, he tossed me in the car, got in the front, and started the engine. That's when I got the door open and pushed myself out. I hit the ground and ran." At her shiver, Brody slid his arm around her. "And you know the rest."

Taking his cue, Foster said, "You said you woke up when you were upside down and he was carrying you out of the building to the car?"

"Yes."

"How long do you think you were out?" The detective's very deliberate use of odd phrasing set off another warning bell for Brody.

"I don't know. Not long? I panicked." Shannon frowned. "It feels like I blinked. We were in here, then we were out there."

"But you don't remember when he bound your hands." The detective pressed.

"Why does it matter?" Brody pinned Foster with a hard, disapproving stare. "You're trying to get to a point, so get there. Faster."

With a nod, Foster pointed to the front door. "Zip-cording her wrists? Ten maybe twenty seconds if she were still struggling, far less because she wasn't. It's no more than ten feet from here to the door. Maybe another twenty feet to the car parked across the street. Carrying one hundred and thirty pounds, I could do it in a few seconds. So, less than a minute from grabbing her to out the door...."

"You think it took longer." Brody frowned. "Why? What have you gotten off the letters?"

"It could be days before we have the full report." Unfortunately, forensic science didn't function in real life like it did on television. "As for taking longer, yes. I think it did. But the question is what was he doing? He didn't kill Bates. She was bleeding out on the floor. Gut wounds are a bitch of a way to go, but they're also slow."

"He didn't want to kill her," Shannon said in a soft voice. "I'd shut down, he could have gotten me out and to the car and been away before I stopped freaking out, but he hesitated over leaving Katrina...."

Foster snapped his fingers. "Exactly. I checked with the 9-1-1 operations center. They had two hang-up calls within seconds of each other...about five minutes before the call from the club you ran to."

Fuck. Brody blew out a breath. "He thought about calling an ambulance...."

"Hang up calls?" Shannon frowned. "Did they come from here? My landline?"

"No, the number was the same on both and traced back to a burner." Foster shrugged. "But it's a good sign."

Brody agreed. The man may have planned it down, but he'd hesitated to kill Bates outright, and he'd considered calling for help. That he ended up doing neither meant he was conflicted—or at least he'd been the night of the kidnapping attempt. Taking Shannon...had it been part of the plan? Or a spur of the moment decision? "What about the content of the letters?"

"Definitely male in tone. Definitely has some kind of education, enough apparently to use correct grammar and punctuation. Obsessed—" Though Shannon had seemed to withdraw into herself, Foster still lowered his voice. "—with Shannon *and* her work. One of the psych workups suggested he has a problem with the military in general and likely you in particular."

That made two of them. Brody definitely had a problem with the guy in question. "I think we should take a break from this and let her get back to work." Shannon would think better after she'd carved for a while. If she worked, he could also have a more in-depth conversation with Foster.

He sent Foster ahead of them on the stairs and followed behind her, one step below. Close enough to pull her out of the way and covering her directly. He tossed her keys up to Foster to unlock the inner door, and they followed him into her place.

"What I don't understand is, what was the purpose? Was it to hurt me?" Shannon paused at the top of the steps. "Or take me? Why *take* me?"

"That is actually one of my questions. We went over your financials, you're doing well, but you're not wealthy." Foster stayed three steps ahead of them, and Brody scanned the room. So much of it remained exactly as he remembered—the blocks of stone, the draping, the work tools and tables.

On his last visit, he'd seen dust and some debris from her work—not rubble. Alarm fired through him, and he caught Shannon's arm and tugged her behind him.

Foster drew his gun. "Stay here," he ordered, and Brody nodded, tucking Shannon more firmly to the wall and planting himself in front of her while the detective swept the room.

"Oh, my God," she whispered. The ragged despair in her words confirmed his suspicion.

The smashed piles on every table shouldn't be there.

"He destroyed them."

Chapter Eight

*M*ore people in her place, more cops, more technicians, and through it all, Brody took the lead. Foster cautioned them against touching anything. He and Brody discussed everything in some kind of verbal shorthand, leaving her out of the loop, and for once, Shannon didn't care. The smashed remains of several weeks' worth of work were all she could see. In reality, the practice pieces weren't a huge loss, but their destruction left a bruise on her heart. The rebar driven into Rebel's piece, however, crushed her.

Not only had the vandal chipped away huge sections and slammed rebar into the head, he'd also systematically erased all the fine detail work. Hateful.

So hateful.

"We're going to get a hotel room," Brody said in his soft, deliberate voice. The one that demanded everyone pay attention. It worked, too.

Rousing from her misery, Shannon shook her head. "No."

"Babe—"

She raised her hand, asking him to stop. "No. I'm not running. I've spent the last week scared and changing my life to accommodate this insanity. And now...someone has been shot, and he *destroyed* my work. He dragged me out of here...and even though I got away, he's trying to take it away from me still." Heart pounding, she gulped in a deeper breath of air. She would not cry, damn it. It didn't matter she wanted to rail and to scream and to crawl into a hole—hell, she wanted to crawl into Brody. Let him take care of it all.

He would. He'd fight her battle, he'd deal with all the people, and he'd keep her as safe as she allowed him to. The son of a bitch who'd done this had violated her life, not once, not twice, but repeatedly.

"Shannon." Brody closed the distance between them and wrapped his hand around her nape. The motion offered comfort and support. God, she could afford to sink. Brody would never let her drown. But doing so wasn't fair to him. "It would be *safer* for you."

"Physically, maybe." She didn't disagree with him. "He destroyed them, Brody. He came in here, and he destroyed what I made. Maybe he didn't rape me, but it...it's pretty damn close. I ran away the last time this happened. And it's still happening. It's like it's happening all over again, and nothing I do is stopping it. I can't control him. I can't control whatever the hell it is he's doing, but I can control me. This is mine. He *can't* have it."

"The last time it happened?" Foster intruded into their moment. "You were attacked before?"

"Leave it alone." Brody's flinty tone was positively glacial, and he pivoted, facing the detective. All that masculine strength and determination in her defense took her breath away.

Foster's expression darkened. From a purely aesthetic standpoint, the detective was a good-looking, if ruggedly handsome, man. But in the intimidation department, he had nothing on Brody. "If she was attacked before, it could be incredibly relevant to our case."

"Leave her alone." The muscles in Brody's arm went taut, and Shannon pressed a hand to his chest.

"I was raped in college." Sickness swam through her at the admission, but her anger painted streaks over the shame. "I don't know by who, I can't give you a description, and I never heard or saw him again that I know of. I was roofied...." Shaking with upset she refused to give into, she continued. "I woke up. I didn't report it right away, and I washed away the evidence, so by the time I did, the cops had nothing to go on."

"Give me the name of the cops you spoke to and where." Foster's tone gentled, and he wrote down the names and the dates. Shannon didn't remember all their names, but the date remained permanently engraved in her memory. "What about who you were dating then?"

"Mostly hook-ups, you know guys I met in class or through the group of friends I hung out with. No one long-term, no one really one-on-one." She knew a few names, but most were not men she'd even seen since before she retreated from the social scene.

"What about after college? Any relationships? Any dates?" Unlike his earlier questioning attempts, Foster seemed to be on her side.

"Jeanine and Henry tried to set me up a few times. They'd ask a friend to escort me, but I didn't...I didn't really like men being around me. I found it too hard to relax or even let them touch me. A part of me always wondered was this the guy who did it? Could it have been him? It didn't matter I'd never met them, I don't remember that night...." Oddly, the normal discomfort she experienced whenever she even thought about the horrible night seemed absent. Maybe she should have gotten angry sooner.

Brody remained vigilant at her side, and he still stood partially between she and Foster, but his expression encouraged her.

"Anything else you can think of? Any disagreements, arguments, disputes you have had with anyone? I don't care if it seems trivial or silly. This," Foster said with a wave toward the room. "This is personal. The anti-military mentions in the notes would seem to be a pointed reference to your relationship with Lieutenant Essex, the destruction of the work on your military pieces, even the attempted kidnapping...it's very focused on you, and controlling you."

Controlling me? "Why would anyone want to? See, that's the part I can't wrap my mind around. I know there're people who don't like the military, and some who think *Her Marine* glorified war—those are two separate things."

"Not when it comes to you, it's not." Brody frowned. Maybe he and Foster saw possibilities where she only found angles. An endless loop or a snake feeding on itself. Obsession had to be born somewhere....

"Before *Her Marine*, everyone pretty much dismissed my work except for some designers who wanted sculptures for gardens or larger downtown projects." She'd actually paid for her loft out of those commissions. Critics panned her work as cold and emotionless. The same could not be said for designers who wanted classical works for their buildings or gardens.

Arguably, she'd taken fewer of those clients in the last two years. The showmanship in her work had earned her a fair bit of notoriety, and she hadn't really paid much attention to it. The work—the love of sculpting and bringing life to the stone and infusing it with all the warmth and enjoyment she'd found in the male form again—had been *her* obsession.

"You've thought of something," Foster said, pulling her attention back to the room.

"Not of anything specific." The butterflies in her stomach stopped rioting, and she blew out a breath. "I've changed a lot of the work I do over the last two years, and I'm taking fewer commissions." Pleasure, not business, drove her once more. "I like those changes. But I'm not going to run. I'm not going to be driven out of here. In fact, if you don't mind, if all of you are done, I would like to clean up the mess."

She wanted to get back to work, stake her claim once more. Flexing her fingers, she was grateful the shaking seemed to have stopped.

It still took Foster and his men another thirty minutes to

clear out, but finally, she and Brody were alone. "You sure you want to stay? We can go get a hotel room, order room service, and you can have a break."

"I'm sure. I'm done running." With repetition, saying it became easier. She was done. "You've been halfway around the world dealing with God knows what. You shouldn't have to deal with this right after you came home. This *asshole* has really ruined what should have been pure fun for us. He's trying to scare me off what I love. I spent five years frozen away, too frightened to embrace what I loved. I became someone I didn't like. I love who I am with you, who you reminded me I can be. I will be *damned* if I let him take it away from me...from us."

"All right, we're going to do a perimeter sweep. Double-check all the locks then we'll go up and clean up. Together. Then we *eat*, and if you still want to work, you work." They had a plan.

"Sir, yes—"

He interrupted her sass with a hard kiss that left her breathless. When he finally let her up for air, he pinched her ass, and she let out a startled laugh.

"I like this bratty side of you." His mouth curved into a slow grin threatening to derail her earlier plans. "You did good today, babe. Real good."

Riding high on his compliment, and his company, Shannon followed him to the doors. Only when he was satisfied, and the alarm engaged, did they retreat back up to the loft. They did a full sweep—checking the windows locks, and ensuring no one lurked in any closet or behind doors. A part of her wanted to tease him for his paranoia and thoroughness, but the confidence she experienced knowing they were secure was a heady relief.

They were halfway through cleaning the debris into crates Brody could haul downstairs later when the phone rang. She didn't recognize the phone number, but the 703 area code said Virginia. "Hello?"

"Hello, I am trying to reach a Shannon Fabray?" an unfamiliar male voice asked.

"This is she." She balanced the phone between her shoulder and ear, so she could open a bottle of water. Cleaning up the mess was sweaty work. Brody had paused when she answered the phone, but resumed work when she gave him an encouraging smile.

"Good afternoon, Miss Fabray. This is NCIS Special Agent Rowdy Easton, I hope this isn't a bad time."

"NCIS?"

The faint twinkle in Brody's eyes vanished, and a fresh strain tightened his jaw. All their hard-earned relaxation disappeared under a layer of tension. Alarm jangled through Shannon's system.

"Yes, ma'am. I'm calling in regard to a Lieutenant Brody Essex...."

Something was wrong. Nothing in his face betrayed his thoughts, but she couldn't shake the feeling she needed to be vague. "Is everything okay?"

"Is Lieutenant Essex with you, Miss Fabray?"

Brody crossed to her, but she didn't give up the phone. Her gut churned. With everything that had happened, she refused to take chances. "I'm sorry, who are you again, and can you verify your identity?"

"I'm NCIS Special Agent Easton, ma'am. And if you'll answer the door, you can see my badge." The sound of the front door buzzer sliced through the silence.

"Hold it up to the camera," she told him and crossed to the monitor in the kitchen. Though the camera had been disengaged when the power had gone out, it functioned fine. The man in the image held his badge up to the camera. He flipped it to the ID, then angled his face, so she could match him to the identification.

"Let him in...." Brody told her in a soft voice. His expression revealed nothing of his thoughts.

"What if he's...?" She couldn't be paranoid when someone

was out to get her, right?

"He's NCIS. I know him." So, a friend. Why then did Brody sound so damn sad? "Let him in." He reached past her and pressed the buzzer.

"Come on up," Shannon told the man on the phone. The agent let himself in, and the locks on the front door reengaged. The elevator hummed as it descended, and the call disconnected. "Brody, what's going on?"

"It's going to be okay," he said, and gave her arm a squeeze.

"That's not an answer." What wasn't he telling her?

The elevator hummed, and she followed him to the cage. The cage door opened, and the man who exited had the same hard cut look to him as all the other Marines she'd met. His perfect posture, neutral expression, and cool eyes demanded attention. A shoulder-holstered gun was visible beneath his suit coat, and he had a pair of handcuffs in one fist.

"Lieutenant Essex."

"Rowdy—"

"Don't, Lieutenant. We're not friends here." But they obviously knew each other, and the exchange seemed to be as much nonverbal as verbal. "You're under arrest, Lieutenant."

"What? No." Shannon cut between them. "He hasn't done anything wrong."

Brody put his hands on her shoulders and drew her out of the way. "Shannon, give us a minute."

"I'm not going to say it again, Lieutenant. You're under arrest. Don't make this more difficult than it has to be." The NCIS agent's voice turned cold and remote.

"Don't be a dick, Rowdy." Brody matched him icy tone for icy tone.

"You're telling me not to be a dick?" Anger seared the words. "You walk off your duty station, leave your men behind, and board a plane for the United States without clearance or leave. You go AWOL, and you're calling me a dick? Criminals do not get to call me a dick. Now, hands behind your back."

AWOL? Shannon forgot how to breathe, and violence electrified the air.

"Give me five minutes, Rowdy." Brody raised one hand. "I don't want to add an assault to the charges, but we may have to if you won't listen to me."

Brody took her place in front of the agent. Her thoughts spun wildly. *How had Brody gone AWOL?* "He had leave scheduled. His team was reassigned, and he applied for leave months ago. He's *not* AWOL." He was one of the most honorable men she knew, he wouldn't....

"I made a choice...a strategic response," Brody said.

"You made a choice?" The NCIS agent's voice grew colder if possible.

"Yes, a choice. Like the choices I made in Fallujah and in Baghdad." Whatever language they spoke, both men seemed to know exactly what was going on.

"Fuck, Brody." The agent shifted his grip on the handcuffs, and the tension-laced air relaxed. "This is serious."

"I'm aware. I have no problem with facing disciplinary action—"

"Disciplinary action? You could go to jail. You walked off a base *in country*, disobeyed direct orders, and abandoned your post. You really think the Military Code of Justice won't be used to ream you a new asshole?"

"I chose this," Brody repeated, and he turned slightly, holding his hand out to her. She grasped it automatically. "This is Shannon Fabray. Look at her."

Agent Easton frowned as he glanced at her, and his expression grew assessing. "What happened?"

"She has a stalker. Three nights ago, the stalker tried to kidnap her. He shot a woman named Katrina Bates, retired Army MP. Shannon got away because she threw herself out of a moving car." Facts delivered in hard, staccato syllables. "He's sent her threatening letters, he's had access to her place, and he's unstable or coldly sane. Either way he's dangerous."

"I'm sorry to hear that." And he sounded quite genuine. "Brody, I can't let you go…I can't let this go."

"I'm not asking you to. I'm asking you for time. Let me make sure she's safe, and then you can take me in."

Shannon's stomach flip-flopped. Arrested. "You could go to jail?" A blow she hadn't seen coming.

Brody cupped her uninjured cheek and stroked his thumb across her skin with a gentle sweep. "It will be okay."

He repeated the sentiment, and her heart believed him, but he'd broken the law. He wasn't supposed to be home.

"Come on, Rowdy." He returned his attention to the NCIS agent.

"I owe you, I know. But I can't break the law."

"Not break, bend. I can't leave her unprotected. I *won't*." Violence hummed through the air like a promise. "If you can't…walk away. Walk away and forget you found me."

"Right, because no other NCIS agent is going to check your girlfriend's place first to find you. The only reason it's me here instead of someone else is because a friend of a friend recognized your name and called before they put a BOLO out." Despite his words, Rowdy Easton didn't appear particularly happy about the subject. "I can't pretend I don't know where you are."

The muscles along Brody's arms went taut, and his shoulders tightened. He would attack his friend to stay with her. *No.*

"Agent Easton." Shannon drew the man's attention to her. "I don't pretend to understand what a decision this has to be for you. But Brody isn't wrong. Whoever this man is, he broke in here while I was gone for the last two days after the kidnapping and while the police were still treating it like a crime scene." She pointed to the rubble she and Brody had cleaned up. "He destroyed my work. The military-oriented pieces and only those."

Rowdy studied the worktables and then her, and finally Brody. "Fuck." The handcuffs disappeared back into his pocket, and he pulled out his cell phone. Dialing a number, he put it to his ear, and Shannon's heart punched at her ribs. "Kim, it's Rowdy.... Yeah, thanks for the heads-up on Essex. I've got a lead, and I'm going to chase it down. How long before you have to make that BOLO live?"

All the tension seeped out of Brody, and he blew out a breath. The men locked eyes, another one of those wordless pulses of conversation passing between them.

"Got it. Yeah, I know I'm asking a lot. But the stupid bastard took a bullet for me and pulled my ass out of a firefight I shouldn't have walked away from." His mouth tightened. "I'll call you as soon as I have a lead.... Yes, Agent Wakefield, I do realize you're bending the rules for me...." For a split-second, laughter edged his words. "Yes, I also realize you'll make me pay for it later. Thanks." Disconnecting the call, he glanced at them. "We have forty-eight hours."

Fifteen minutes later, an unhappy Shannon settled in front of her stone. She'd turned on the music, but how she could hear over the water and the chisel, he had no idea. Anger—and hurt—simmered beneath her confusion. She didn't understand, and she might never, but he'd deal with the fallout when it happened. Not before. Ignoring Rowdy, Brody tackled the kitchen, and it didn't take long for the agent to strip out of his suit jacket, roll up his sleeves, and go to work helping him.

"She's pissed at you."

"Not your problem." Her anger was actually a good thing. Despite the fury in her eyes, she'd not retreated from touching him. Hell, quite the opposite. She'd dug her fingers into his hand and slapped his chest. She'd allowed herself to be a victim for a long time.

"So, give me the details on the man harassing her."

Appreciating the bluntness of the request, and needing to focus on something other than Shannon's disappointment, he answered Rowdy's question. By the time he'd finished reciting the last of the known details, the kitchen was clean and they'd brewed a fresh pot of coffee. Brody had given Shannon a cup in one of her sealed mugs, so she didn't risk getting stone chips in it.

"How the hell are you planning to catch this guy? You don't know who he is. He hasn't tipped his hand other than to escalate to extreme violence swiftly. He may not try to take her next time, you know. Maybe next time, he just tries to put a bullet in her."

The possibility drove Brody. He had to control the circumstances of the next encounter.

Rowdy wasn't finished, however. "Do you have any suspects? Somewhere to start?"

"No. Look at her. She doesn't have a mean bone in her body. Whoever this guy is, he has to hate her to do what he did. You didn't see her face when she saw her work destroyed. I've seen hell in someone's eyes before. I never want to see it in hers again." Killing the son of a bitch who hurt her wouldn't give back what the man had taken, but it would assure he never took from her again.

"What about the rape in college?" Rowdy pitched his voice low, even if Shannon couldn't hear them.

"Nothing to go on. No reason to believe it's related." As soon as he had a target, he could move on it. But he needed a target.

"No reason it's not, either." Folding his arms, Rowdy leaned against the counter with his back to the room.

Unlike Brody, Rowdy had a huge family to fall back on—a Navy family. They'd been displeased with his choice to go Marine. He'd met Rowdy on assignment, and they'd served together on a handful of occasions. Well over a year before, Rowdy had taken early detachment and gone NCIS agent. He approached the world from a different angle, but that still didn't explain the statement. "What the fuck are you talking about?"

"You're assuming what happened in college doesn't have

anything to do with now. But what if it does?" He cocked his head to the side, his eyes distant and thoughtful. "One of the agents I work with handles cold cases primarily. She always says 'walk it backward, when that doesn't work, walk it forward.'"

"Still not following. Shannon doesn't remember the guy, reported the case without any DNA evidence, and basically only has what she remembers from the morning in her place."

"Her dorm room, right? So, what was out of place there? How had she known she'd been raped?"

"Because she didn't have her panties on." Just rehashing the case caused his blood to boil. The night he met Shannon, he'd seen the echoes of her old hurt. Shadows of pain marred her eyes and limited her ability to trust.

"And?"

"And what?"

"The guy didn't wear a condom. Now, college guys aren't the poster children for safe sex, but the guy took the time to plan a roofie, so why not wear a condom?"

The automatic response of, "he's an asshole" couldn't be the one Rowdy reached for.

"C'mon, man. You're too close to this. These days, guys don't wear a condom for three reasons—careless, thoughtless or...?"

Brody studied Shannon. The intensity of her focus on the project in front of her kept her preoccupied and away from their discussion—emotionally as well as physically. She'd relaxed.

"He trusted her." The guy hadn't just met Shannon at some party.

"I'm going to bet if we pull apart her life over the last few years, we're going to find a pattern." Rowdy continued speaking, but Brody only half-heard the words. The guy dropped a roofie in her drink, raped her, and left the next morning. Shannon didn't report the rape right away, and by the time she did, the police had no physical evidence to work from.

The case had gone nowhere. She hadn't confided in anyone, other than a therapist and her agent, until she'd met Brody. The nature of the notes was possessive and anti-military—or were they anti-Brody?

"The guy trusted her because he *knew* her. She withdrew from her life, changed a lot of it...and *forgot* about him." Which had probably been okay, until Shannon began to really make a name for herself.

"We need to question her about her college life—who she saw, what she did—everything before the rape."

"I'll do it." No way in hell would he allow Rowdy to dig into her life.

"You are way too close to this."

They needed to establish some ground rules. "You bring it up to her, you try to press her for details about a time in her life where her faith in herself and her trust in the people around her was ripped away and left her fundamentally changed to the point she still has PTSD issues, I'll kill you. Clear?"

"It's not going to be any easier on her coming from you." No, it wouldn't be, but the difference between him and Rowdy was Brody loved her. He'd already gotten inside her defenses, and he wouldn't destroy her just to get to the truth. "But you don't want my opinion. I'll take first watch. Four hour shifts?"

"That works. Rowdy? Thanks."

"Yeah, you're welcome, and I don't fuck my career for just anyone. Let's make this count."

Brody waited, taking a seat to watch her sculpt. Maybe he was giving himself time, hell, they both needed a break. After thirty minutes, she shut off the water and the music and shifted to face him. "You lied to me."

"No," he said, but he didn't offer excuses. "I let you assume my leave came through."

"Brody." She started to reach for him but stopped herself. Uncaring of her wet, work-dirtied hands, he grasped them.

"You're career military. You could go to jail."

"Probably will." He shrugged. "Doesn't matter."

"How can you say that?" When she would have jerked free, he drew her closer.

"Because you *needed* me."

"I need you to not be in jail."

"Yeah, I need you to be alive and to feel safe. I wasn't able to do either there. Here I can be effective."

"And when they arrest you?"

"Doesn't matter right now."

Her nostrils flared. "It matters to me."

"And *you* matter to me." Elbows resting on his knees, he leaned into her. "You can be pissed at me later. When this guy is nothing but a blip in the rearview mirror. I promise to stand still while you tear a strip off my hide. Until then, we're doing this *my* way. Understood?"

Her mouth tightened, and his gut twisted. If she rejected him at this point, it would suck, but he would handle it. Finally, she relented. "I'm not going to 'sir, yes, sir' you. We're not in bed."

Scooping her up, he marched her around the silkscreen dividing the room and dropped with her on the bed, pinning her. "You were saying...."

"Brody, I'm filthy."

"Those are not the words I'm waiting for." This was what his life had been missing. Playfulness, arguments—make-up sex.

"Sir, yes, sir." She laughed, and he covered her mouth with his, thrusting his tongue in to enjoy the taste and sound of her. Touching her was always a revelation; she gave everything to every interaction, her kisses as greedy and demanding as they were giving.

Loving her was the best thing that ever happened to him. With reluctance, he broke the kiss and nuzzled the corner of her mouth. "I need to ask you some questions, sweetheart."

"Okay."

"About your life before the rape."

She stiffened, but he kept close. The dilation of her pupils and the hitch in her breathing were both fear responses, but she dug her fingers into his neck.

"You can hold onto me," he told her, encouraging the behavior. "I will not let you go. You're not going to be alone. But the only person who was there, who can tell us what we may need to know, is you."

"You think this guy...the one who took me...is the same man who raped me?"

"Rowdy has a point. Bad things happen to good people." God, did he know they did. "But we can't ignore the possibility."

Her throat convulsed with a hard swallow, and she closed her eyes, seeming to hold her breath. When she opened them, she whispered, "Do we really have to talk about it?"

"Yeah. No one has to know anything. Just me."

"Brody, I wasn't always that great of a person...."

"I don't care about who you were, sweetheart. The words you need to be saying right now...?" She could do this, he had faith in her. She had to know it and believe.

"Sir, yes, sir." Her grimace belied the words. The fact she said them at all was enough.

Chapter Nine

The lock of his mouth on her nipple sent electric shocks of pleasure through her. Somehow, strip questioning hadn't been what she'd imagined when he said they had to talk about her past. Bristle along his cheeks rasped at her skin, adding another layer of pleasure. Brody took his time, nuzzling one breast then the other. When he resettled next to her on the bed, he leaned on one arm and continued to trail his fingers from her chest to her abdomen.

"You went to college to study art, didn't you?" So *not* pillow talk, and she wanted to object, but he'd said they needed to know. The lazy path he blazed left tingles in its wake. Remembering the details would be hard enough, but it made the feelings associated with those memories even more elusive.

"I went to a charter for high school, and I'd been in a pilot program for the school district for years. The art charter school was similar to the pilot program. It focused on my strengths. I was a very visual learner." Her thoughts derailed when Brody undid the buttons on her jeans. "We still had all the same types of classes, but they taught them differently. In English, we did read, but our projects weren't necessarily papers or only papers. Instead, we did paintings, sketches, comic books...."

She'd loved her school. "Science fairs were art fairs with a scientific theme, and even math classes weren't just standard formulas but designed to create something. Most of the students at the school were just like me. We reveled in what we could create, and in my junior year, I did my first sculpture." Heat bloomed in her belly, unfurling like a flower stretching up to the sun. Brody continued to explore her skin, and she could almost imagine the color trailing behind his fingers across her flesh.

If she worked in oils and canvases rather than stone, she would love to try and recreate his actions. "Anyway," she said with a shudder as he circled the tense point of one nipple, never quite touching. "I worked in cast plaster. We had a guest artist who came to the school. Greg was in his late thirties, good-looking and talented." She peeked at Brody's face when she said good-looking. His mouth quirked, and a hint of amusement slid behind his studious expression, but he didn't comment.

"He worked in plasters and created busts. He had all these fancy ones of famous actors and actresses...." She rolled onto her side to face Brody and tugged at his shirt. If he wanted to play touch her and drive her mad, she wanted to do the same to him. The corded steel of his muscles was hot under his fingers. "Come to think of it, Greg even had a bust of Lauren. Huh, I'd forgotten about that. Anyway, he taught some guest classes, and it turned out I could do what he did pretty easily, but more than the skill to do it. I *enjoyed* sculpting, the feel of the knife working on the softened plaster, carving it to the shape I wanted."

What a revelation it had been. Drawing, sketching, paper mâché, painting, chalks—she'd liked all forms of art. But sculpting? "It made my soul sing." At Brody's raised eyebrow, she laughed. "On the first day of the charter school, the principal told us art should come from the soul, and when you find what makes your soul sing, you should embrace it. I thought it sounded too pretty...almost ridiculous. But I was fourteen then, and almost seventeen when I met Greg, so I didn't really understand what the principal meant until then. When Greg's guest classes were done, he gave a few of us his number, and I called him. I wanted to learn more about sculpting, and he offered to give me some private lessons."

She kept her gaze on Brody's abdominals. The washboard cut of them, the way the muscles tensed under her touch, the light sprinkle of hair extending from his belly button to disappear beneath his jeans.

"You slept with him." The rumble of his voice vibrated against her fingers.

Embarrassment flooded her, and her face warmed. "Yes. He was amazing and talented and so focused. When I was with him, I felt like the center of his world. The affair didn't last long, thankfully. I fell for him but not the other way around. When I went to college, I really wanted to focus on my art and making something of myself. I also wanted to...." She paused to explore the thick welt of an old scar just below his pecs. Whiter than the skin around it, the bulge protruded above the surface of his skin. "I wanted to experiment, so I fed my muse however I could, partied, drank, danced...."

"Seduced a lot of college boys, did you?" No judgment echoed in his words, and when she dared to peek, none reflected in his gaze. If anything, his lips hinted at an indulgent smile.

Emboldened by his support, she nodded. "I went a little crazy. I liked sex. Not just for the act, but the intimacy. They were hot, fast little affairs. We'd burn up the sheets for a few days, and then I'd throw myself back into my classes. The relationships, if they could even be labeled such, didn't last very long. This feels so weird telling you about these men."

"You aren't telling me about them. You're telling me about you." Well, that didn't sound so bad. "I do need you tell me about them. The men you slept with, and the guys you dated. Who was important in your life then? Who were your friends? Who did you hang out with?"

She didn't answer immediately, choosing instead to explore a fresher scar pebbling along his side—the grated cheese effect—he hadn't had this before. If she asked him, Brody would shrug it off, but if she really wanted to know, he would tell her. It was how it worked between them. When he tucked his finger beneath her chin and nudged her gaze up, she sighed. "I don't really remember their names. Their bodies—yes. I remember one guy had a good smile, another had dimples. But they had swimmer builds, all long and lean. Another one was more muscular, I think he wrestled or maybe he was on the football team." Who they were hadn't really been important.

"As I recall, my body fascinated you, too." The teasing note had her blushing, and she felt like her scalp had to be on fire.

"I knew your name, and I've never forgotten it, but...." This time she frowned and sat upright. Brody followed her, continuing to stroke her arm. "But you weren't the first guy I tried to go out with. They fixed me up twice before. One of those guys was someone I knew in college...Don...Dennis...Darrin.... I don't know, it started with a D." The name seemed right on the tip of her tongue. "He had a softer build. Nothing really cut about him, but his muscles were there. He always made me think of the nerd hero you read about in books. Like he was one workout montage away from buffing up."

Brody hummed, the sound a cross between amusement and disapproval. The sound of it echoed in the vibrations under her fingertips.

An unsettled feeling coiled in the pit of her stomach. The brush of Brody's knuckles passing down her side to her hip seemed distant, like he touched someone else. *D-something...brown hair, hands...something about his hands...and he....*

"Shannon, come back here. What's going through your head?"

He'd carried her out to the car. The cool rain splashed her.

His shoes squelched on the pavement with wet slaps. Her face hurt from where he'd squeezed her mouth. Her wrists ached, and blood rushed to her face. The pulse of her heart seemed to echo in her ears. Every step, his shoulder cut into her stomach, and then she landed on the seat—the leather seat. The car smelled of rain, leather, and burnt popcorn. God, she hated the smell of popcorn on its own, much less burnt.

The man who'd shot Katrina slid into the front seat and started—

"Shannon." Brody shook her, the force snapping her to the present. She lurched off the bed, away from him, and barely reached the bathroom before she threw up. He followed her, and she held onto the edge of the toilet as she emptied her stomach. The water turned on and then off. A moment later, he draped a cool washcloth over the back of her neck and smoothed her hair away from her face.

Trembling seized her as though she were still being shaken, and her stomach roiled all over again. The water came on again, and then Brody reached past her, flushed the toilet, and closed the lid before he urged her to sit on it.

He had to help her hold the glass.

Brown hair...he had brown hair. His hands were rough, and he'd smelled like.... Her gorge burned a path up her throat. She shot to her feet, and Brody had the toilet open for her and held her hair when she vomited again. Behind her the water turned on again then the shower, and when Brody stripped her out of what was left of her clothes, she let him pull her under the spray.

Hot water spattered her—the force more than the splash of rain. He didn't let her go. His skin seemed hotter than hers, or maybe her hands were simply icy. The masculine scent of him filled the humid air, but the cloying burnt popcorn seemed permanently lodged in her sinuses...burnt popcorn and damp, musty.... Her mind shied away from it. God, she didn't want to remember.

Burying her face to Brody's chest, she tried to blot out the scent memory with the present.

"Talk to me," he ordered, keeping his arms around her. Unlike her, he still wore jeans, but he didn't seem to mind the water soaking him. "You remembered something. What was it?"

The hand clapping over her mouth—the scent of it. She'd wanted to throw up. She would never forget the smell. Only she had...until now. Not wanting to recall it, she'd shoved it out of her mind. And water sliding down her neck. Cold dripping into her soul.

Leather seats.

Damp, mustiness.

Burnt popcorn.

"Plaster," she whispered. "It's a sour odor, like rotting eggs when it's wet. I smelled plaster."

Brody held her chin in his hand, tipping her head back so the water cascaded over her hair. Hell, if not for him, she'd collapse right there in the shower. "Like the man you had an affair with in high school? Greg?"

"No." Greg's hair hadn't been brown. "He had this reddish-blond hair, almost coarse, and kind of curly. The man who broke in here had brown hair."

"You didn't see him, sweetheart. He grabbed you from behind." No disbelief, just a confirmation of facts.

"In the car...." She swallowed hard. "I saw him in the car. His profile. The lightning kept flashing. His hair was brown, and he...." The world swam. Bands of pressure squeezed her chest. She couldn't breathe. Flashes illuminated the inside of the car. He started the vehicle, and he—

A hard kiss forced air into her, and she clung to Brody, fighting through the flashback replaying in her mind with violent intensity. "You shouldn't," she told him and tried to pull away.

"Why not?" He raised his brows.

Shannon groaned and settled for giving him a closed-mouth kiss before drawing back. "Because my mouth tastes like ass."

"You say potato, I say po-tah-to." A terrible joke that wasn't even particularly funny, but she laughed anyway.

"He hummed, Brody." Saying it aloud made it real. "I heard him hum when he started the car, and I remembered hearing it before."

"Not Greg." The hot water continued to pour around them. Despite the steamy heat and his nearness, she was so cold.

"Not Greg." She confirmed and then dug her fingers into his shoulders. "Dale Weston. His name was Dale Weston, and he was in one of my life studies class. He didn't have an artistic bone is his body for creating new, but he excelled at replicas. They expelled him the same year...he'd been copying other students' work and selling it."

"Babe, I'm not following."

"When Jeanine fixed me up with him, I didn't remember him...barely remember him now." It wasn't because he'd been unremarkable, far from it. From the moment he'd picked her up for dinner, she'd been uncomfortable. She'd wanted to make her excuses and leave him at the curb but had promised Jeanine she would try. "I told her I would do it because I needed to get back out, I needed to stop running. She said he was a nice guy, bland and unthreatening...and he liked my work. She told me he'd seen me at an opening. Never mentioned which one, but it should have been a red flag."

Brody shifted her to the wall, and she leaned against the cool tile. "This is the D guy you couldn't remember." Always clarifying, assuring his facts.

Shannon nodded. "I don't want to talk about this anymore. I don't want it to be real."

Lathering his hands up, he began to wash her arms, and she let him. She wanted to run away. "I know you don't, sweetheart. But you're not there anymore, and you've been running for a long time. You don't have to run now, but you do have to tell me."

"You're going to think less of me." Hating how small she

sounded, she fumbled for her earlier anger and failed. Dale had taken her to an Italian place because she loved Italian food. How could she have been so stupid? At no point had she mentioned her likes or dislikes. He'd brought up Florence and her exchange program. Shannon didn't talk about that with anyone.

The whole meal had been uncomfortable; she'd barely touched her food. Finally pleading illness, she'd gone to the bathroom. Once there, she'd called Jeanine and told her she couldn't do this. She needed a ride home. Jeanine talked her down from her fear, talked her into giving it one more shot. When she'd gone back to the table, he had his back to her...and he'd been humming.

Reciting the story in a wooden voice, she barely felt Brody washing her, but the movement of his hands kept her grounded. Every time she thought she began to slip off into the dark place, Brody was there, anchoring her to the present.

"What did you do?" Again, he threw her a lifeline.

So, there she'd been, standing in the Italian restaurant, and the song he hummed slammed into her like a physical blow. One she experienced all over again in the back of the car. Terror spilled into her veins like a virus, destroying everything in its path. "You know those zombie movies where they pile on top of each other, this seething mass of violent death, pawing, scrambling, and clawing their way to the surface, and you know they're just going to keep coming, and nothing you do will stop them?"

Brody nodded and maneuvered her under the water to rinse off the soap. The tension drained away, and her muscles went lax. She was a doll. Brody could manipulate her however he wished, so unlike anyone else in her life. She trusted him. Really *trusted* him. Even with Brody pushing her to face the memory, she had fled full throttle for years, she wanted to do it for him.

For her.

"It all rushed over me in one moment, and I remembered

the night I'd forgotten. I remembered him touching me and not being able to do a damn thing about it." A hard lump formed in her throat. "I just laid there, and he grabbed me and touched me and grunted, and I didn't want him to, but I couldn't even find the strength to push him off me. When he finally stopped, I just remember being glad it was over, and then I closed my eyes. I wanted to forget it happened—pretend it never did." Everything in her revolted, and she tried to drag air into her lungs. "He was humming when he left my room."

The same song he'd hummed in the car.

The same, almost cheerful tune he'd hummed in the restaurant.

"I ran. I turned around, walked out of the restaurant and never went back. I lost my shoes somewhere, and I was running barefoot. I caught a taxi and went back to my place. I locked myself in, and I didn't come back out." She'd been out on a blind date with her rapist. "I didn't tell anyone because I thought...it was crazy. That I was crazy. I didn't go out with anyone again...not till the night I met you."

"Shannon." He said her name in the softest whisper. His face swam in her wavering vision. Tears she didn't even realize she'd been shedding slipped free with every blink. "You beat him, babe...you got him out. He's held you captive for years, and you fought him. You got away. He's *never* touching you again."

"Do you hate me?" She didn't know if she could stand losing Brody. "I went out with him. I recognized him, and I didn't report it...*twice*."

"Shh, how can I hate the other half of my heart? You were a POW, even seeing the open gate you didn't believe it. It happens. But you're not in that cell anymore. I'm here, and we're getting out of here together, okay?" His arms tightened around her. "Hold onto me, babe."

"Brody?"

"Yeah?"

"I love you." Shaken to her core, she chipped away the

debris she'd all but buried her heart in. "I love you so much."

His fierce grin housed joy. "I love you, too."

Cold, quiet rage seethed beneath his skin, and the urge to hunt one "Dale Weston" fired across every nerve ending. However, he couldn't—wouldn't—leave her in in this moment. Nor could he resist touching her. Her admission of love filled in all the dark, empty spaces in his soul. The more he knew her, the more he loved her.

From experience, he knew how soft her skin was, but he needed to touch her and taste. Unwilling to wait longer, he stripped off his soaked jeans and shut off the water before wrapping her in a towel and carrying her back to the bed. Setting her on her feet, he kept her steady. Slipping a hand over her shoulder, he indulged himself. Damn, she was softer than silk.

Her shiver of reaction vibrated through him, and he took his time, drying her with deliberate motion. Shannon didn't pull away; instead, she kept reaching out to touch him. The need for contact, and the tremulous smile despite the dark revelations and the flashbacks, struck him hard and fast. She'd tried to shut down on him but had listened and hung onto him when he stayed in her space.

More, she'd said she loved him.

"Brody." She exhaled his name with a groan. He continued to towel her dry, stroking every inch of her skin. The bruises were still dark and angry, but the scrapes were healing.

"Are you hurting?" Despite all the bumps, bruises, and shocks, he hadn't seen her take anything.

"A little," she admitted and gazed at him.

Running his hands along her legs, he reveled in the muscle beneath her satin flesh. "You're gorgeous. Do you have any idea how beautiful you are?"

Her nostrils flared, and the small smile on her face grew. "I always feel beautiful with you."

"Good." He pressed a kiss to her tummy. "Hurting,

however, isn't acceptable."

Laughter trembled in her voice. "No? Are you the boss of me?"

"Absolutely." And he meant it. She belonged to him. He'd teased her earlier about understanding she was taken. He'd held onto every communication, every whispered sigh, every memory they created...and he wanted more. "I love you." He didn't need to repeat himself, but he chose to anyway. "I'm not looking for Ms. Right Now or a good time or a fling."

With his tongue, he drew a circle on her tummy and then dipped lower. Dropping the towel, he cupped her ass and held her steady when she began to sway.

"No?" Strangling the single syllable, she placed her hand on his head. No pressure, no weight. Merely a touch to help her balance. The trust in the simple act smashed his resolve.

"No, I want more. A lot more." Massaging her ass, he remained mindful of her bruises. Everything about her went softer, more relaxed, and she drifted forward, and her knees buckled. Lifting her, he set her on the bed. "From the moment we met, you intrigued me."

"I was a mess. I'm still a mess," she protested. He bent and bit her nipple gently—hard enough for her to feel the sting, not so hard as to hurt her.

"Be nice to my girl," he told her before laving the spot he'd nipped. He'd known from the first week what he felt for her went beyond simple attraction. She had him itching from the inside out. Some women might have used the success she'd found in her sensuality to look closer to home or experiment, but not Shannon. The nascent bond they'd formed deepened, and she hadn't merely relied on him to chase away her demons.

She'd confronted them on her own.

"Life is messy," he said, delivering the words between kisses. "Chaos exists in everything we do. You're strong, and you own who you are."

"How do you always know what to say?" No longer content

to be passive, she cradled his face and traced his features with her thumbs.

He pulled himself out of his musings and back to the woman who turned his life inside out and made him a better person. "Do you have any idea who I was before I met you?"

"No." The simple answer caused him to smile, but she wasn't finished. "But I have a good idea. You're kind, and you're smart, and you're incredibly loyal. You never had anyone before the Marines who showed you a kind of loyalty in return. You don't expect things from other people, and you're genuinely surprised when you receive them. You live to defend, to fight and make this a better place. You would have gone home with blue balls the night you met me if I hadn't wanted you enough to overcome my fears...but wanting you has never been a problem. You always put me first. Sometimes it scares me."

Possessiveness he'd come to associate with her slapped him upside the head. The same urge to claim her had been a fire in his belly since their first night. She was right , and no matter how much of his Neanderthal side it appealed to, he kept the decision in her hands. Too many other choices had been taken away from her.

"It will always be your choice," he said, fisting her damp hair and dipping down for a long kiss. She met his tongue stroke for stroke. Shifting, she spread her thighs, creating a place for him, and cradled him closer. "I want you, permanently." She needed to know this wasn't an affair or a fling, or something he would abandon. "But it will always be your choice."

"I chose you," she said, tugging him until his forehead rested on hers. "I *love* you."

"Be sure," he said, fighting the very primitive urge to just take her at her word and to hell with the consequences. "I mean it, Shannon. If you want something else—" He wouldn't say someone else because then he'd be battling a far more violent urge to kill that mysterious someone. "I would understand. I'm a Marine. I'm not sure where the next assignment will take me, if I don't end up in jail. I know we talked about me retiring, but it might not be an option. Everything I have, everything I can give you, I will...but sometimes, I can't control what they demand of me." Or where they demand he go. She'd needed him once, and he hadn't been here.

He trailed his fingers over her curves, unable to lie there and not touch her.

"I am sure." And with her whisper, she'd both freed him and shackled him willingly. "I don't want anyone else. I don't even like other people the way I like you. I *love* you. I choose you. I will always choose you. Everything else we can figure out."

"I'm never letting you go." Offering her a last warning on a last chance he would never make good on. He'd been hers from the first day, and it was his privilege to keep her.

"Promises, promises...." A gleam of humor chased away the shadows in her eyes, and she arched her back, rubbing her breasts against him. One kiss had never been enough, nor had one night. He'd known for a long time.

A lifetime wouldn't be enough. "Marry me?" His benefits would be hers. His guys would look after her if he couldn't. She'd have his name, and worst-case scenario, he could move her onto a base. She'd be swimming in Marines; no one would ever get near her again if she didn't want them there.

Tremulous smile growing, she wrapped her arms around him and rose to nuzzle his mouth. "I love you, Brody. Yes...I'll marry you."

He teased his tongue along the seam of her lips, and she opened them willingly. No hesitations, no retreat. Once he stole inside again, she moaned. The vibrations tingled against his mouth and filtered across every nerve in his body.

She didn't even hesitate for a second. She was perfect. Generous breasts tipped with hardened dusky nipples. Long, gorgeous legs that didn't quit. Smart. Sassy. Vibrant and passionate in her responses. She held him with strength and offered him her vulnerability—and more—she gave him her trust. He poured his want into the kiss, and cupped one breast so he could play with the tip.

Conversation was over. He continued to kiss and suck her tongue for several, long panting moments before abandoning her mouth to dip lower. Her harsh inhales and groans offered up her pleasure like a fine meal. Nothing shy in her response, nothing held back, and the scent of her arousal acted like a drug on his system.

Fuck, she owned him body and soul. He grazed his teeth over her nipples, sucking one, then the other.

Sliding his hand down her belly, he shifted so he could reach her sex. She was wet and warm, and he knew how it would feel to thrust his cock into her. He circled his thumb around her clit. Her arms tensed, and she moaned, long and low. No, she didn't hide her pleasure from him or fight her own responsiveness.

He eased two fingers into her, soaking up the pleasure in her gorgeous eyes. Where she'd been pale and haunted before, she flushed. So pretty and pink. He pressed on her clit, and she cried out. He wanted to play and make her come in so many ways, but the lust in his veins exploded. Playing would be for later, he'd wanted to lay claim to her so deep and hard she'd never doubt who she belonged to, where he belonged.

He rose for another taste of her mouth, enjoying the way her inner muscles clung to his fingers and how she dug her hands into his shoulders and then his sides. She didn't pretend not to need him as hard as he did her, but she didn't drive him to do more either.

The surrender of her pleasure to him so utterly was the sexiest thing he'd ever experienced. She was an absolute joy to behold, a delight of curves, fragrant skin, and the most provocative sounds. A perfect fit for him.

"I want to take my time." He had to grind the words out, past the clawing beast demanding he satisfy them both immediately.

"No, you don't." She defied him with a breathless laugh. "I'm not going to break, and you don't have to prove anything. I want you—every day, every way."

She gave him permission to slip the leash, to feed the yearning in his soul that left him so vulnerable. Accepting it, he gave her another hard kiss before rolling free. He needed a condom, and they were in the bathroom, but she stopped him.

"You don't...."

His brows rose.

"I'm on birth control, and even if I wasn't...I'm ready to leap with you."

Permission and invitation invaded his reason. If he got her pregnant, they'd be tied together forever. But who was he kidding?

They owned each other.

"You sure?" Somehow, accepting all of it made teasing easier.

The door in the other room opened, and they both went still.

"Yo, Brody, I'm going to...."

Shannon's eyes grew into big circles, and she bit her lip, amusement vibrating through her in suppressed giggles.

"Get out, Rowdy," he yelled in response, not bothering to disguise his growl. "You come back up here before I let you know you can, and I'll kill you."

"I'm going to get coffee and talk to you later." Laughter trailed the man out, but the stairway door closed, and a lock tumbling closed echoed behind him.

The heat of her sex warmed his cock, causing it to twitch. "Fucking bastard." But the last came out without any real censure, and he settled along Shannon once more. "We can have kids whenever you want, but I'm a greedy man, and as much as I want my baby in there, I want you to myself for a while."

"Like I said, I'm on birth control...and I don't want

anything between us."

He couldn't argue, and he didn't want to. No more delays. No more interruptions.

No more separation.

He moved back between her legs. When he gazed at her, he forgot how to think. How had he ended up so lucky? All her dark hair spread over the sheets. Her lips swollen from his kisses, and her dark eyes heavy with the same lust devouring him—perfection. One more slow, easy kiss had his heart pounding and his need burst out control. He rose up to his knees, pulled her hips up and then entered her in one, hard swift movement.

Fucking hell. It was the only thing that came to mind. Not exactly romantic, but it was what it was. Nothing kept him from feeling every silken, hot inch of her. Her muscles tightened around him as he pulled himself out and thrust once more. Shannon thrashed her head from side to side. Her hips arched, eager and demanding, meeting him motion for motion.

Impatient, and wanting her pleasure nearly as much as his own, he slid a hand between them and worked her clit. Between one instant and the next, she convulsed and screamed his name. Her orgasm had her inner muscles clamping down on him, pulling him deeper, and he slammed into her. It didn't take much before his spine went white-hot, and then his own orgasm took over, and he came hard and fast.

Her second orgasm pulled him farther into her warmth, dragging his from him. One last thrust, and he lost it. His balls dragged up hard, and he came with a shout. Collapsing, he fought to keep from crushing her, but Shannon had no such reservations. She wrapped him up in her trembling arms and legs.

"I love you, Brody." She brushed a kiss to his ear.

"I know." He wore a small smile, felt a giddiness more suited to a schoolgirl than a Marine flowing through him. "I'm keeping you, Mrs. Soon-To-Be-Essex."

"Oh," she said with a startled laugh that had her inner muscles flexing around his softening cock, and the sensation twisted his insides. "I love the sound of that."

"Me, too." He didn't mind admitting it. *Wife.* She would be his. His to take care of. His to protect. His to keep for all time. Rolling over, he pulled her with him and settled her like a feminine drape across him. Shannon snuggled closer and rested her head on his chest. She couldn't disguise her drowsiness, and he began to rub her back in slow, gentle circles.

Sleep. She needed to sleep.

And Brody needed to plan.

Dale Weston's days were numbered. He just hadn't realized it yet.

Chapter Ten

"When did those two get here?" Brody asked while watching Jazz Cavanaugh, along with two women he hadn't expected to see again, take the elevator up to Shannon's loft studio and apartment. Sergeant Mary Phillips and Corporal Roxy Cortez had both been members of Jazz's FET team in Afghanistan. The last time Brody had seen the other two women had been when his team went in to get them out and facilitate transport before sweeping the town for insurgents.

Logan and Zach had brought all three with them when they'd arrived to take over watch, so Brody could head out with Foster and Rowdy. They had an appointment to see Dale Weston.

"Roxy and Mary are both assigned to Quantico for a few months to teach some training classes, and they had some leave, so they came to see Jazz." Zach's smooth answer earned a snort from Logan.

"What he's not saying is Roxy's husband decided his wife's regular deployments meant he needed to fuck around on her. He's also suing her for custody of their kids, and she's a wreck. Mary brought her here, so Jazz and she can buck her up."

Shit-ass situation and not the first time a deployment had come between a married couple. "That sucks."

"Yep," Logan said with a nod. "But we have three Marines

up there with your girl, and all women. Keeps her comfortable and safe." He didn't need to add it kept Jazz safer by extension. Neither Logan nor Zach would let Jazz take on a potential combat situation without backup.

"Thanks, guys." And he meant it.

"No problem. We'll be here." Zach motioned to the first floor. "We got this. Just get the son of a bitch."

"Oorah." Brody had every intention of getting the son of a bitch. A knock on the door indicated Foster's arrival. With Rowdy following, Brody headed for the door. Shannon was as safe as he could make her for the moment. After today, she wouldn't need to worry about Weston again.

"Sorry I'm late." Foster's brusque tone made a mockery of the apology, but Brody didn't care.

"What do you have?" He hadn't slept the night before. Instead, he'd held Shannon and waited. When the nightmares came, he'd cuddled her, chased them off and made love to her. Sex wasn't the answer to everything, but it damn sure helped. By the time dawn arrived, she'd gone into a dreamless sleep, and he'd left orders to let her sleep until she woke. He'd sent a text to Foster about Weston and talked to Rowdy about it over coffee in the middle of the night.

"Dale Weston is a nobody. He does a lot of craft shows on the weekends and otherwise lives pretty unremarkably." Foster flipped through his notebook. "Unmarried, he has an apartment about a mile from here. He's been turned down for membership at the Sybarite Club four times. He's been trying to get in for the last two years."

"How the hell did you get it?" Rowdy had his phone out. "There's no public listing for a Sybarite Club."

Foster smiled tightly. "He's got a very chatty neighbor. Sixty-five-year-old busybody who doesn't like him. Weston freelances as a graphic artist, gets assignments from a few employment agencies here in town that provide creative marketing specialists. Like I said, pretty unremarkable. But one of the guys at the station did an Internet search...seems

Weston also freelances on the web, does graphic design for people and sells some really stunning replicas."

Angling his phone, Foster held up an image. *Her Marine* jumped out on the screen. Statues modeled after it, anyway. The work didn't seem as refined. Brody squinted and then took Foster's phone to enlarge the image. In Shannon's work, the face had clearly been him. She'd even added the scar near his eyebrow and the dimpled scar he'd gotten from chicken pox.

Weston's work didn't look like Brody at all. The features were softer and lacking real definition. "He's changing it enough so it appears close but isn't the exact same." Whether it was to disguise his rip-offs so he could say they were inspired or simply because he lacked her talent, Brody didn't care. His work invaded Shannon's gift.

"Yeah. He's got a lot of her stuff on there. I checked with her agent. She went through the site and said nearly every independent piece he sold was based on something your girl did. The earlier stuff is almost a carbon copy. Her more recent work, including that piece, has a surface resemblance only." Foster's mouth twisted. "The problem we have is this is the only evidence I can dig up on him being a douche bag is this. Her agent said they'd contact a lawyer to try and shut him down, but I can't find anyone who is a witness to his actions. Lots of circumstantial...Shannon's questionable memory."

Brody lifted his gaze from the image and glared at the detective. "It's not questionable. She remembered a scent, a hum, and his hair."

"I believe you. I believe *her*. It's not enough for a jury. On cross-examination, a defense attorney would shred her. She didn't report the rape until days later. When she encountered the guy again, she didn't report it a second time. Now, all of a sudden she remembers? It's too convenient." Foster held up his hands.

"He's a cop, Brody. You can't kill him." Rowdy's cool tone carried a hard edge. "He's not wrong. We don't have the evidence, but we do have a suspect. We dig hard enough, we'll find something."

"When did he try to join the Sybarite Club?" The exclusive, members-only facility was the first place Brody had met Shannon. He'd gained admittance on Luke's recommendation. His former captain and several of the Marines at Mike's Place were members. In addition to the live shows and burlesque atmosphere, the club also had rooms in the back and playrooms for those with the predilection for anything and everything.

"The same night you and Shannon had a date there. The club keeps records, and the manager is a friend." Foster had to be a member, or he'd never have gotten the details. Leaning on his car, the detective scanned the street. Almost no foot traffic came through the area this early in the day. The shops around the corner didn't open until after ten. "Bates is awake. She's groggy, but they're moving her out of ICU. I brought her some images to check and slipped a photo of Weston in."

Brody sighed. "She couldn't ID him."

"No." To his credit, Foster didn't bother to hide his disappointment. "Morgan was still on watch there, and we're keeping a plainclothes station at the hospital. Weston doesn't know she can't ID him, so there's a chance he may still come at her."

"It's not her he wants," Brody said, quietly.

"Actually—" Rowdy claimed Foster's phone and studied it. "—it's not her he hates. He wants her, sure, but he doesn't hate her."

"What does that have to do with anything?" the detective asked before Brody could.

"Look at the big picture stuff...this jackass has been copying her work for years. If she's right, he also raped her in college, but they didn't even *date* then. Later, he's fixed up with her and she takes off, doesn't call him again. He's still copying her work, but then her work changed." Rowdy raised his brows and stared at both of them as though expecting them to follow his logic. "He's obviously not able to copy the new stuff as well. What was in those letters she received?"

"The military angle," Foster said. "He wanted her to stop sculpting military men."

And he'd broken into her place and smashed all of her practice pieces. The loss had devastated Shannon.

"Right. If he's the same guy who was in her room in Boston, he went after something the night of her big opening there. The only damage she reported was to her sketchbook." Where she drew out her ideas, tried to envision what she wanted to create. She'd spent hours sketching Brody on the night they met. She still sketched him, telling him once it relaxed her. When he'd asked her to carve a piece about Rebel, it had thrilled her.

The challenge. Shannon had reveled in the challenge of capturing all the men he'd served with, in stone, because they were all different. His first date with her—she'd come because she wanted to recapture....

"Passion." Brody wanted to swear. "Shannon's work changed two years ago because she recaptured her passion. This fucknut thinks it's the military work. It's why he wants her to stop. He wanted into the Sybarite Club because it's where she and I met. He probably thinks something inside affected her. Has he been stalking her since college?"

"If he has, he can't hide the evidence of that. But to get a search warrant I need cause, and right now, we don't have it." Foster sounded pissed off. Another point to him.

"Then we get evidence." Locking him up wasn't the only solution to their problem. The man had hurt her—too many times.

"We can't kill him," Foster said.

"No, we can't," Rowdy agreed with the detective. "He doesn't have to know we can't."

"Yeah, we're *not* torturing him either. We keep digging, and if the guy is guilty, we will find what we need to lock him up." The system. The detective wanted them to trust the system.

Cold rage surged through Brody's veins and then quieted. His respiration and heart rate settled. He'd run headlong into places most men were pissing themselves to get out of. He'd gone in, done his job, and been successful more times than he'd failed. Fast response was what he did—his anger had to wait. "I don't need to torture him. I just need to taunt the fucker. I'm not waiting for him to slip up or to try for Shannon again. He's been doing this for years. All he has to do to not get caught right now is to wait us out." To wait out the clock running on Brody. Rowdy had given him forty-eight hours. Less than thirty-six remained.

"You want to go see him." It wasn't a question, and Rowdy didn't bother to hide his disapproval.

"Oh, yeah." Brody smiled. "Where is he right now?"

Less than an hour later, Foster led the way into the Chase tower. Weston's current assignment was only six blocks from Shannon's studio. Apparently, the bastard liked to be close to her. They took the elevators to the thirty-second floor. Both Foster and Rowdy wore suits, Brody stood out in his jeans and T-shirt. A vicious part of him wanted to put on his uniform, but he didn't currently have the right to wear it and might soon lose all rights to it. So, he'd do this as the man, not the Marine.

Only two companies dominated the floor, one that managed oil and a second that handled advertising and public relations for a broad spectrum of clients. Foster produced his badge and told the receptionist they were there to see Weston. The woman picked up the phone quickly and called her boss. Within minutes, they were led to a conference room, and Weston came in from another door.

The man focused on Foster then Rowdy. Their suits suggested authority, and the delay gave Brody time to study his target. Nearly six feet in height, his brown hair cut with military precision, leaner build, but he'd apparently been trying to build bulk, based on the muscular neck and forearms.

He had a softer build. Nothing really cut about him, but his muscles were there. He always made me think of the nerd hero you read about in books. Like he was one workout montage away from buffing up.

So, the man had found his workout montage. He might even be able to take a real beating. Brody didn't smile.

"Detective, they said you needed to talk...." Weston's gaze found Brody, and his genial, bland expression fled. The man blanched, and sweat appeared on his forehead. Not saying a word, Brody stared at him.

"Yes, we have some questions regarding a case we're investigating." By the book, Foster had insisted and Rowdy agreed. The two cops wanted to play it straight and clean. They wanted to be able to arrest the guy. Brody hadn't disagreed on the latter point, but as to the former, he was open to interpretation. "You are Dale Weston? You attended the University of North Texas and later, the Dallas Art Institute?"

Weston didn't answer immediately, and if it were possible, he paled further. Dark circles stained the underarms of his dress shirt. Caught between fight and flight, the coward stood there, with a dumb expression on his face, and stared back at Brody.

Fear. Weston needed to feel it. How many years had Shannon been locked into a cage this son of a bitch had the key to?

"Mr. Weston?" Rowdy took a single step in the other man's direction. Weston fell back three, damn near hitting the door he'd entered by. "Can you answer the question?"

"What—" Weston coughed and jerked his gaze from Brody to the other two then back. Brody didn't smile, and he didn't give the man a moment's respite. The sweat practically dripped down Weston's face by then. He fought to recover, but he couldn't stop glancing at Brody. "Why do you need to know?"

"Just answer the question, Mr. Weston." Foster didn't give an inch.

"Fine, I went to both UNT and the Art Institute." No reason to offer a denial. While Weston remained pale and sweaty, he also seemed to be fighting to recover from his shock. "If that's all you needed, I have work to do."

"Sit down." Rowdy tapped the table. "We have a few more questions."

"I'm sorry, this is where I *work,* and I don't have to answer anything." There, the sniveling little weasel had found his courage. "If you want to talk to me again, call my attorney, Martin Fisk. I'm pretty sure you can find his number with a search."

"I said *sit down.*" Marine training came in handy, and Rowdy's orders had an effect on their target whether the other man liked it or not. Weston took two steps toward the table before catching himself and stopping.

"Mr. Weston, we're investigating a series of crimes," Foster said. "So, you can feel free to not answer our questions right now, which would constitute an obstruction of justice charge and we can take this conversation to the station." Which wouldn't do any of them any good unless the bastard confessed. If they had enough evidence, they wouldn't even need this conversation. Foster would have arrested him.

After a long exhale, Weston gave them a tight smile. "Ask your questions."

"What's the nature of your relationship with Shannon Fabray?"

Weston waited a beat too long. "Who?"

Rowdy pulled out a copy of the college paper and set it on the table. The lifestyle section featured a photo of Shannon and Dale standing side-by-side at an art fair. How the hell Rowdy discovered the information, Brody didn't know.

Making a show of examining at the paper, Weston couldn't quite hide the faint tremble of his hand. The perspiration ring under his arms grew larger. The men had rattled his cage.

But not enough.

"Apparently someone I went to college with," he lied. "Do you know everyone you went to school with?"

Foster set another stack of papers on the table. "These are from your website, StatuesForYou dot com. Interesting how each and every one of the *replicas* you're peddling bears a striking resemblance to Fabray Originals."

Each sheet contained the images of Shannon's work next to Weston's. Brody hadn't needed the evidence of how good or how much better her work was than the cheap knockoffs Weston produced.

"Wow. What do you know? She sculpts Greek statues?" His air of cockiness couldn't diminish the stink of his body odor. "Because no one else does."

"And *Her Marine*?" Brody asked, speaking for the first time. Weston's attention jumped back to him, and the other man swallowed hard. "Everyone sculpt this one, too? Of course, her work is exquisite. Detailed. Incredibly accurate and evocative. Passionate."

Weston reacted to each adjective as though they were physical blows.

"And yours?" Brody sneered. "Pretty pathetic, cheap, and a lame effort to copy a master."

Chin jerking upward, Weston scowled. It was an ugly expression, and hate filled his eyes. Brody smiled. *Come and get me, fucker. Give me a shot.* He'd put him down faster than a rabid dog and without as much kindness.

Weston jerked to his feet. "I don't have to stand here and be insulted. What does my work have to do with a police investigation? It doesn't even justify a copyright infringement."

Oh, he thought he had power now, particularly because he'd stopped pretending he didn't hate Brody.

"Fine." Foster took on a placating tone. "If you can just tell us where you were three nights ago between the hours of six and ten."

"Why?"

Foster smiled, and it wasn't pleasant. "Because I asked. Answer the question. Where were you three nights ago between the hours of six and ten in the evening?"

Rowdy's phone buzzed. Pulling it out of his pocket, he glanced at the screen. "Mr. Weston, do you own a Glock?"

"I was at home and yes. I own a handgun. I have a license." The muscle in his jaw ticked again.

With a hand on his own gun, clearly visible at his waistband, Foster eyed the other man. "Do you have the handgun with you?"

"I— No. It was stolen." His eyelids twitched, and the sweat dripped off the tip of his nose. "A few days ago— I mean a few months ago."

"Did you report it?" Foster remained congenial, but Brody had seen a similar attitude in investigators before. They would even smile when they clapped on the handcuffs.

"No. I know I should have, but I was pretty busy at the time, and you know, I couldn't...."

"Uh-huh. How was Boston last week?" Rowdy wasn't through with him either. "You flew via American Airlines from DFW with a layover in Chicago going, and Charlotte returning. According to airport footage, you were also sporting some bruises." Rowdy turned his phone around.

God bless NCIS. Rowdy's partner had come through for him, and Brody hadn't even realized they'd gone at it from that angle. No way DPD pulled surveillance photos from an airport so quick, but NCIS would have been able to get to them faster.

"I fell." Weston lied, and he slid his left hand into his pocket. "Now, if you'll excuse me, I'm pretty done with your questions. You want me, you talk to my attorney." He stormed out, and they let him walk.

"He's guilty as fuck," Foster said flatly. "How soon can you get me surveillance for his trip to Boston?"

"Not long. Kim's working on it right now. And that's three favors I owe her." The two men continued to discuss it, but

Brody tuned them out.

He had a target. He knew the man's face, his address, and the type of gun he used. Everything else was simply a confirmation. Dale Weston raped Shannon, stalked her, and tried to kidnap her. Brody had once offered to break the man's legs.

Brody always kept his promises.

Shannon perched on a stool next to the bar leading to her kitchen, hugging her mug of coffee and listening to the chatter of women who laughed, teased, and gave each other so much shit. Maybe they were Marines, but they acted the way any old friends hanging out would. Their feminine laughter echoed through the studio. All three women were there when she woke, and Brody was gone. The sleep had been wonderful, but worry still nibbled away in her gut.

He had left with Rowdy and Detective Foster to confront Dale Weston. Coldness slithered through her veins. She'd recognized him. All these years, and she'd never been able to put together the pieces of that night. But both times she'd come into contact with him, she'd known. It left her sick, and yet...relieved. The relief confounded her. Images flickered through her mind, playing like some bad film reel with the sound cutting in and out.

"Hey," Jazz called out, her voice slicing through the memory. "It's going to be okay." All of the women stared at her, but it was Jazz who rose and walked over, with what had once been a pronounced limp still in evidence. Admiration filled Shannon. Compared to what Jazz had gone through, her problems didn't seem so bad. "You're kind of a hero, you know."

"Oh, hell," the dark skinned woman—Mary or Stormer, or maybe both—said with a long laugh. "Do not inflate her ego."

The blonde Latina grinned. "Just because she landed two gorgeous men who practically worship the ground she walks on doesn't mean she's a hero."

Mary snorted. "Ground she walks on? Did you forget Jazz walks on water?"

Jazz merely responded by giving both women her middle finger and then leaned against the bar next to Shannon. "Ignore them. They're high on leave right now. Soon, they'll be back to work being useful to society." Despite it all, Shannon couldn't help snickering. At the sound, Jazz's smile grew. "See, that's how you face all the bullshit that life throws at you. Laugh at it and say, 'do it again bitch. I've got this shit.'"

"Oorah," her friends chorused.

"I've never been good at laughing in the face of anything...always thought I was something of a mouse." She ran, she hid. When Shannon had had the chance to identify her rapist, she'd fled again and buried the information so she didn't have to confront it. "Not so much a hero."

"No one is," Jazz said, soberly. "None of us. We're survivors. We live. We love. We go on. Heroes are for storybooks and fairy tales. Life is a fuck-ton harder."

"I should be doing something." What, Shannon had no idea, but simply sitting there in her loft didn't seem productive. Brody had come halfway around the world to help her, and he'd endangered his career to do it. She owed him more than merely waiting.

"You *are* doing something." Mary rose and headed into the kitchen. She refilled her coffee then held up the carafe as though asking if Shannon wanted more.

Extending her mug, she gave her a small smile of gratitude. "I'm waiting and drinking coffee. I don't really think this counts as doing something."

"You'd be surprised. You're safe, so Brody doesn't have to worry about your security. You're here for when he comes home. You're alive, and it makes him happy." When she phrased it that way, Mary sounded sensible.

"Waiting is the hardest part of the job," Jazz said, her manner still quiet and intense. "The guys had to wait for me, and it drove them crazy. Spouses, children—families wait for their Marines to come home. It's hard. Harder when they don't come back, but you can't *not* be here. If you're not up to this, know it now. Brody will go back."

If he didn't end up in jail. Her Brody, in a cage. The mere idea hurt. "I would wait till the end of time for him."

"Then you're doing something." Roxy joined her friends and got a refill for herself. "In the Corps, you learn a lot about hurry up and wait."

Living her life in standstill hadn't been near as hard as waiting the long months between Brody's deployment and return, but nowhere near as rewarding either. "How did you do it?"

"Friends." The answer from all three happened almost simultaneously.

Jazz chuckled and then held out her hand. They'd all been so careful about touching her even as they hugged, punched, and generally leaned on each other. "You have friends. You have *a lot* of friends. We're all here for you. If you'll let us."

Lauren was her friend. She'd shown up one day after meeting Shannon, having decided they were going to enjoy each other's company. Their friendship had been nurtured by Lauren's own pushiness. Zehava at the community center was her friend, too. A friendship borne from common interest. And Liam had all but adopted her. So many of her friendships were because the other person wouldn't take no for an answer and accepted her, quirks and all.

"Let us?" Mary scoffed. "Hell, girl. We're here period. You try and get rid of a Marine who doesn't want to leave. You're stuck with us. Besides, I totally want to see you carve something out of one of those stones. Kyle is a huge fan, and he's going to go bug-eyed jealous when I tell him I met you."

Hand still extended, Jazz raised her brows.

What did Shannon have to lose? *Nothing.* And everything she'd gained with Brody? All the people she'd met because of him? "I'd like to be friends."

"No take-backs." Mary covered their joined hands.

"No do-overs," Roxy said, and for a moment tears glimmered in her eyes and vanished again.

"No tears." But despite the order, Jazz released Shannon to give Roxy a hug. "No more tears for that bastard."

Mary rapped her hand against the counter top. "You know what this calls for, right?"

"Liquor or ice cream?" Jazz chuckled. "I can't drink at the moment. Too many meds."

"Ice cream it is." Mary'd already turned to the fridge.

Shannon frowned. "I don't have any—"

"No worries." Jazz pulled out her cell phone. She hit a single contact for speed dial and wagged her brows. "Hey, babe, we have an ice cream emergency here and four grouchy women...." Whichever husband she'd called said something, and Jazz laughed. "What flavors do we want, ladies?"

Within thirty minutes, they all had big bowls of ice cream, spoons, and had dragged together the various chairs from different spots to create an impromptu sitting area. Despite her worries, Shannon hadn't laughed so hard in awhile. When the door burst open, she'd almost forgotten the women were there to guard her. Mary and Roxy hit their feet so fast and were between her and the door, she'd barely had time to process they'd moved.

Foster entered with Rowdy and Logan right on his heels.

"Is he here?" The NCIS agent demanded.

Shannon's heart sank.

"Back off," Mary ordered, and Rowdy scowled.

"I need to know if Brody is back here or if he called."

They'd lost track of him.

"We got that," Roxy said slowly, her tone cool and unimpressed. "But you don't need to burst in and scare her. Brody's not here. We haven't seen him since you left this morning."

With trembling hands, Shannon pulled out her phone and checked it. No missed messages.

"Shit," Rowdy said and rounded on Foster. "He had to go

after him. You got the address?"

"What part of 'don't scare her' do you not get?" Logan thumped Rowdy, and the agent glared, but then he gave her an apologetic smile. Whatever they said next was too low for her to hear. Shannon didn't care about the apology.

What had Brody gone to do?

Chapter Eleven

*D*ale Weston's speedy arrival home wasn't the least bit surprising. In fact, the man was a little late by Brody's estimation. Brody'd had time to let himself in, search Weston's desk, studio, and bedroom. All of the evidence sat in a neat stack on the coffee table. Evidence Weston was likely desperate to destroy. Unfortunately for him, Brody had documented every bit of it by location, and worn gloves to remove it from their hidey-holes—not that he'd had to *find* the photo of a nude Shannon.

One he didn't plan for anyone to see. The presence of her panties and other photos would be incriminating enough.

The echo of the door slamming reverberated through the house. Weston rushed into the living room, then stumbled to a halt. Seated in a chair, Brody braced his knuckles together.

"You have no legal right to be here," Weston said, the warbling wobble in his voice not doing him any favors.

"Nope. I don't. Go ahead and call 9-1-1. Report a break-in." Brody smiled. "I'll wait."

The waste-of-fucking-air had no ready response. Sweat beaded his forehead, and his already stained shirt darkened further. His gaze turned wild-eyed, and he glanced from Brody to the coffee table to the kitchen. While he didn't look at the door, he shifted his stance, and his body practically trembled.

Would he go for his gun? Could the gutless piece-of-shit be desperate enough yet?

Raking his hand over his hair, Weston blew out a breath. "What do you want?"

Apparently not desperate enough. *Pity.*

"To kill me?" Weston demanded when Brody didn't respond. "Or maybe you just want to scare me." He swallowed once and glanced down at the table. "None of this is admissible. You don't have the right to be here. I've seen those cop shows. It all became tainted the minute you walked in the door." A pause, and the fucktard let out a laugh. "You fucked yourself, man. You broke in here for nothing."

Brody still said nothing, the force he exerted pressing his knuckles together ground bone on bone. The pain in that kept him grounded.

"Fine," Weston said, gesturing to the table. "I'll stop copying her work. There, you happy? I said it. I copied her work. I'm an asshole. But nothing I did was close enough to be illegal. I always added my own personal touch."

Brody waited. If he stood or released the leash on his temper...no. Surgical strikes required patience.

"Why are you just sitting there?" The man took a step toward him then paused and rocked back on his heels. "Are you wired? Trying to get me to admit to something?" Another bark of laughter, though it sounded more like panic than amusement. "I copied her style of work, recast in inexpensive plaster, and sold it. Made plenty of money. I don't really need her stuff anymore." Then with an almost sly gleam in his eyes, he smirked. "That's all I've done."

Brody dropped his hands and stood. Weston held his stare for a scant few seconds before beating a hasty retreat toward the door. The sudden, sour stink of ammonia gave Brody a reason to smile.

"Fear," he said, softly. "Hurts, doesn't it?"

"I'm not afraid of you," Weston lied and shifted in the direction of worktable lining the wall next to the kitchen. He twitched and changed direction to head for the landline. Grabbing it, he wielded the handset like a weapon. "I'm going to call the cops. You're not supposed to be here. You're supposed to be in Afghanistan. I did my homework. You're breaking the law even being in the United States. I bet your military cops are looking for you. What are you going to do then? You'll be in prison. Not me."

"Go ahead. Dial the number." Brody walked to end of the coffee table, and Captain Jackass hit the wall in his rush to back up farther. His loud panting filled the silence. "Do you need me to dial it for you? Fear response can increase adrenaline, respiration, and heart rate. It also shuts down nonessential functions. Your bowels tighten and cramp, your bladder empties—although you've taken care of one already. Vision and hearing are enhanced, so is the sense of smell. Memories become far more potent, but fortunately, so does your resistance to pain. At least initially."

Weston's eyes widened, and his knuckles were white against the phone. Now, he let his gaze slide to the door and then back to Brody. He probably wondered if he could reach it before Brody got him. What were his chances?

"Fight or flight," Brody continued. "It is the body's natural response to aggressive stimuli. Fight and kill, or run like hell and try to live. Most predators, they go for the fight. In the animal world, it's pretty basic. Now that I think of it, it's pretty basic for humans, too. Prey, however.... Prey only knows how to run unless it's cornered and given no choice whatsoever."

The phone dropped with a clatter. "I'm not going to fight you. If you attack me, it's assault and you're just racking up the charges. You're a trained killer. That makes you a deadly weapon. Texas has the death penalty."

"I haven't done anything wrong," Brody said softly. "Yet."

Anger collapsing into confusion, Weston twitched. "Then what are you doing?"

Pathetic. Like every other bully before him, the man couldn't handle someone who could fight back. "Having a conversation. What are you doing?"

His nostrils flared, and the whites of his eyes became even more pronounced. A vein throbbed in his forehead.

Brody lunged forward, stopping well short of the man. "Boo."

Weston screamed and dropped, covering his head with arms.

Disappointing, really. The vicious little terrorist was weaker than the woman he'd victimized. "Not so threatening now, are you?"

"Just leave me alone, I'll do whatever you want. Just leave me alone." He practically sobbed the words.

"You want me to leave you alone?" Brody studied him, and because he never pretended not to possess a sense of viciousness, stomped his foot. Weston jerked, dropping his arms, and slammed his head on the wall with a very satisfying crack. Pain creased his forehead, and hatred flashed in his eyes.

"If you're going to kill me, just do it already," Weston screamed, and like any animal pushed into a corner, he struck out. Brody caught his fist and twisted his hand, bending the arm in a direction it wasn't meant to go. His second scream rose on a ragged note and then went to a whimper. He tried to strike with his free hand, and Brody caught it, then delivered the same treatment. Fucker pissed himself for the second time.

"Do you know how much pressure it takes to break a bone?" He kept his tone conversational. "How if you apply it correctly, you can snap it in two places? Standard bone breaks heal pretty well, joints on the other hand...." Increasing the pressure, he studied the man's face as it mottled red and his breathing came in rapid-fire gasps. "Some pain can be so intense, it shreds your ability to think and form coherent sentences. Your nerves report something is wrong to the brain, it sends a signal like an SOS. Your thalamus gets the message, and then farms it out. Sometimes it even crowd-sources the signal to figure out what is the pain, where did it come from?"

Weston's eyes rolled back, so Brody switched the pressure. He let him have a few seconds of relief. Weston sagged, and then Brody caught his thumbs and bent them backward. A fresh scream tore out of his target's throat.

"Your brain asks, is it sharp? Have I felt this before? Is it better or worse than something else I did? For example...." Slamming Weston's left hand to the wall, he heard one of the knuckles crack and the man whimpered. "Better or worse than your thumbs being screwed? What about your arms? Better or worse? Did you know not every pain makes you cry? The limbic system decides. Fascinating shit. It's why physical pain and emotional pain can cause the *exact* same reaction...and how torture can be so very effective."

Releasing him, Brody rose. "Your heart rate increases. You sweat. Respiration increases, and your brain fights to keep up with all the input coming at it. Of course, they say to help alleviate one pain, you send the brain a new signal." Placing his foot on the man's knee, he began to exert force and Weston's eyes bugged out. "Emotional and mental pain are the same way. You keep hitting the same set of nerves, they're going to eventually shut off or develop a tolerance for it, so you have to create a worse one to get the brain's attention. Tell me, Dale. Do I have your attention?"

He made a sound, it might have been a word.

"I'm sorry," Brody said and leaned down, increasing the force applied to his knee. "What did you say?"

Weston gurgled. "Yes...you...have...God, it hurts!"

"Good." Straightening, he removed his foot from the knee. "Take a moment, catch your breath."

"You're fucking insane." Curled in on himself, Weston remained flushed, and tears wet his cheeks.

"Whine less. You're still breathing." That could change. Brody glanced at his watch. "Time is nearly up, Dale. So pay attention. I won't repeat myself. You're going to confess. You're going to tell the cops every single thing you did, then you're going to plead guilty and accept whatever time you're given."

"Why would I?"

Letting every emotion drain out of his voice, Brody said coldly, "Because if you don't, one night, when you think you're safe, when you think everyone has forgotten, and nothing bad could happen...you're going to see me. It will be the last thing you see, and when I bury you, it will be in a very deep, very dark hole where no one will hear you or find you again. You're going to beg me to kill you, but death would be too kind."

Brakes squealed outside the house.

"Do you understand, Dale?"

With a hard swallow, Weston gave him a defiant look. "I don't believe you."

Outside, car doors slammed.

"Wrong answer." With one hand, he hauled Weston to his feet, and with the other, he handed him his gun. The man stared at the weapon stupidly, and the door burst open. "This is going to hurt."

Foster came through the door first, gun drawn, with Rowdy following. They both spotted the gun, and Brody field-stripped it. The pistol went to pieces in his hand. He kicked, connecting with Weston's knee. The sickening crunch of bone split the silence, and Weston went down with a wet scream. Taking a step back, Brody raised his hands and met Foster and Rowdy's gazes evenly.

"Self defense."

"You crazy son of a bitch," Rowdy muttered. He holstered his sidearm and approached Brody with handcuffs. Foster followed in his wake, cell phone in hand, requesting a bus to the address for Weston. He paused when he caught sight of the coffee table and all the evidence of stalking in plain sight.

Understanding registered in Rowdy's eyes, but it didn't diminish his anger. Brody allowed him to handcuff him. "Lieutenant Essex, you're under arrest for violating Article 86 of the UCMJ. Under Article 31, you have the right not to incriminate yourself, no one has the right to question you without declaring the nature of the accusation, no statement may be made under coercion or inducement, and no one evidence *unrelated* to the charge will be compelled before a military tribunal. Do you understand?"

"Yes." But he didn't go into cuffs alone. Foster read Weston his rights and shackled him as well. Brody didn't shift his focus from Weston, and though the man wept, he looked away every single time his gaze collided with Brody's.

Mission accomplished.

Thirty-six hours later at Quantico, Brody stood at sharp attention, facing Colonel Linda Edmond in a courtroom occupied by the judge and two other JAG officers—Navy Lieutenant Terrance Mills for the prosecution and Marine Captain Mitch Thomas for the defense.

"Lieutenant Essex, you are being charged under Article 86 of the UCMJ, absence from your unit," the judge said, examining the papers in front of her. "Do you understand the charge?"

"Yes, ma'am."

"According to the statement you gave to NCIS, and later repeated to Colonel Jessup, you left Camp Leatherneck of your own volition, with no assistance, and flew to the United States in order to assist your girlfriend with a personal issue?"

"Yes, ma'am."

No emotion disturbed her expression, but she glanced up from the papers to study him. "Has the issue been resolved, Lieutenant?"

Oh, yeah. "Yes, ma'am."

"According to a statement filed by Special Agent Easton, you surrendered yourself when he contacted you with regard to your failure to appear." It wasn't a question, so Brody kept his mouth shut. "I also have statements here from Congressman Sparks, Lieutenant Colonel Tom Baxter, Captain Luke Dexter, Gunnery Sergeant Jasmine Cavanaugh, Sergeant

Ryan Brun, Sergeant Mary Phillips, Corporal Roxanne Cortez…. The list here is rather extensive, Lieutenant. You apparently have quite the fan club."

Still no question, so Brody remained silent. The judge didn't appear disapproving or even curious. She seemed…bemused. Only the sound of papers shuffling filled the room, and finally she set them aside. "Captain Thomas has filed your statement and intention to plead guilty to the charge. Is that your intention, Lieutenant?"

"Yes, ma'am."

"Very well, Lieutenant. This court-martial accepts your guilty plea and commends you on taking responsibility for your actions. As you intended to return to your duty station and took no action to avoid being returned, and you were absent for seven days, you face confinement for six months and forfeiture of two-thirds pay, per month, for six months."

He'd expected the sentencing, and was glad Shannon had remained in Dallas as he'd asked. His only regret had been not being able to see her before Rowdy hustled him onto a plane. It had been the best decision. Federal custody reduced the chances the DPD would charge him with assault.

Weston, on the other hand, confessed before they even got him to the hospital. Rowdy dropped him a note via Captain Thomas. Weston faced a pretty decent set of charges.

Shannon was safe.

"Lieutenant Essex, your contract is due to expire in ninety days. You filed for leave, and you haven't signed a new contract or filed an intention to renew your contract. Were you planning to renew your contract?"

Moment of truth. "Undecided, ma'am."

His response gave the colonel pause. "Explain, Lieutenant."

"I've served for nearly fifteen years, ma'am, the majority of which I was deployed. Afghanistan, Iraq, Afghanistan again, Turkey, Kenya, Iraq, and most recently Afghanistan again. The Corps is my family, my father, my brother, my sisters, and my mother. I am proud of my record and my service. My only regrets are the brothers and sisters I wasn't able to bring home, but based on my recent decision-making, I believe I am compromised and question whether I will be as successful in future service as I have been in my previous." A hard truth, but he'd chosen Shannon over duty. He'd tested the argument while he'd been twiddling his thumbs, awaiting his orders to return to the States and to a well-deserved leave, instead of in the middle of a firefight or in the back hell of beyond—but had word reached him there of Shannon's predicament, he couldn't say he wouldn't have made the same choice.

"A commendable concern, Lieutenant. And if your discharge was delayed and your contract not allowed to expire?"

It would delay his seeing Shannon, but she'd said yes to marrying him once. They'd make it work. His woman was strong. "I would obey the order, ma'am."

"With prejudice?" Was she asking as a part of his sentencing or out of honest interest?

"I'm afraid I don't understand your meaning, ma'am."

"If I ordered you to serve out your confinement then report for duty and reassignment without leave, and without the expiration of your service contract, Lieutenant. What would be your response?"

"Yes, ma'am." He had no other response.

"You have ninety days to decide, Lieutenant. Until then, you are confined. Your pay will be docked by two-thirds for the next three months. Your promotion to Captain is on hold. I expect your answer before the ninety days is up. At that time, we will discuss whether you will serve an additional ninety days. Understood?"

"Yes, ma'am. Thank you, ma'am." He snapped a salute. Ninety days confinement and docked pay—it was a slap on the wrist.

The colonel rose. "Off the record," she instructed the court reporter, and the corporal ceased typing immediately. "I cannot credit you for absenting yourself from duty; however, I can applaud your honor and dedication to your girlfriend."

"Fiancée, and thank you, ma'am."

"Congratulations, Lieutenant. Court dismissed."

Chapter Twelve

Three Months Later

*W*hen Brody's uniform had been delivered first thing in the morning, the corporal in charge of the delivery saluted and informed him Captain Thomas waited for him in a conference room. Other than an hour each day in the exercise yard that Brody spent running, and a weekly trip to a barber on base, and one specific visit with Captain Thomas a month earlier, Brody had spent the entirety of his confinement in close quarters and alone. Dressed, he finished packing the last of his clothes into a duffle and double-checked the room was neat before exiting to find the corporal and sergeant awaiting him. Both men snapped into attention at his arrival.

He nodded to them. "At ease."

"Thank you, sir. This way." One led, with the other falling into step behind him.

Brody would not miss the empty walls and simple rooms of the facility. Considering he'd had access to running water and a rather comfortable cot, he couldn't complain about the accommodations either.

Inside the room, Captain Thomas worked on a file while waiting for Brody. Assuming attention, Brody saluted the captain. "Lieutenant Essex reporting, sir."

"At ease and good morning, Lieutenant." Thomas rose, stretched out his hand, and smiled. "We'll keep this brief."

Clasping the other man's hand for a brief shake, Brody nodded. "Morning, Mitch."

"First things first." Mitch swiveled the folder around and slid it across the table. "Your promotion cleared. Sign the bottom line, and you'll receive retroactive pay to the day it was initially filed."

"Minus the two-thirds of the last three months." Not that he minded; he'd worked hard to earn his captain's bars. He signed the paperwork where indicated, and Mitch countersigned it. The ceremony of having his bars pinned would usually be more formal, but Brody had no complaints.

"Congratulations, Captain Essex." Mitch grinned then clapped him on the shoulder.

"Thank you. Do you have the rest of what I need?"

Returning to the file folder, the JAG officer nodded. "I do. Have you changed your mind in any way?"

"No."

"Do you understand by signing this agreement, your discharge will not be complete for another sixty days, and during those sixty days, you are still bound by UCMJ and subject to new orders?"

"Yes, sir." The appellation was automatic.

"You don't need the 'sir' anymore, Captain."

Brody smiled faintly. "Will still take some getting used to...Mitch."

"You've had a minute. Adapt." But he smiled as he said it. "Also, you may be recalled to duty at any time in the next three years. If ordered to report, you will have seventy-two hours to present yourself on base and to your commanding officer. Do you understand?"

"I do." He swallowed the automatic *sir*.

"Sign here." Mitch indicated then began to flip through the papers to the others Brody needed to sign. "Make sure the contact information is correct. You'll have to check in for a change in military ID, but beyond that, you're free to go."

Free to walk out the door. Free to head home. Free to see Shannon.

"Thanks, Mitch." The JAG officer had been assigned to his case, but the captain had listened without judgment to his statement and backed Brody on every decision. He'd also gone above and beyond to handle the discharge papers when Brody informed him of his decision.

"My pleasure, Brody. I don't agree with the AWOL, but I get the reason why. Corporal Barnes out there will escort you to the front." He packed the papers back into his case then paused. "Oh, I saved the best for last. Your ride is here, too."

"My ride?"

"Five foot seven, long black hair, bedroom eyes, and a killer smile?"

Shannon.

Time to go. Pivoting on his heels, he gave Mitch another nod and let himself out. Five minutes and an elevator ride later, he strode out the front doors and into the sunshine. The blaze of summer had passed during his confinement in the box, and the dazzling colors of autumn decorated the trees. How long had it been since he'd even seen those colors?

His interest in them waned swiftly, however, at the sight of the women leaning against a car. Dressed in jeans, a T-shirt, and denim jacket, her hair pulled back into a ponytail, Shannon personified sexy casual. More, her face lit up with a gorgeous smile, and no trace of shadows haunted her eyes. A bulldog sat next to her, his tongue lolling out of his mouth.

"Wow," she said as Brody walked down the steps. "You look amazing in uniform."

"Thank you, ma'am." At the last step, he dropped his bag and opened his arms.

"Stay," she told the dog then rushed forward and launched at Brody. He caught her and held her tight, their mouths fusing together in a kiss he'd waited months to give her. Tears dampened her cheeks.

"Hey," he said against her lips. "No crying. No sadness."

"I'm not sad." She rubbed her forehead to his. "I've been pissed. Frustrated. Turned inside out, and finally, relieved. Right now? Now I'm happy. So these are happy tears."

Accepting her at her word, he set her on her feet but didn't release her. "I missed you."

"I missed you, too." Drawing back, Shannon swiped away her tears and then caught his hand. "Come, I want you to meet the new guy in my life."

He grabbed his bag and followed her over to the car. She crouched to put an arm around the bulldog. He wasn't a puppy, but he certainly wasn't full-grown yet. Setting the bag on the car, he squatted next to them. "Hey there, fellow."

"Brody, Raphael. Raphael, this is Brody. You can say hi." The dog was well-trained because though his body wiggled slightly, he hadn't moved from his seated position until she told him he could.

"Come here." Brody tapped his chest, and the dog leaped and greeted him with a few enthusiastic swipes of his tongue. Laughing, he gave the dog a good scratch between the ears and eyed his girl. Her smile grew as she watched them, her eyes softening. He had to ask. "Raphael?"

"I'm an artist, and he just isn't a Brutus." While Brutus was the name of the USMC mascot, Brody had to agree. "Down, Raphael."

The dog dropped obediently, and Brody nodded. "Nice."

"A gift from Logan and Zach." She laughed. "Jazz said it was to warm my bed until my Marine came home again...but he's also getting guard dog training. The loft has all the latest upgrades to security, and the first floor renovations are ready to go." But it sounded more like a question than a statement.

"You've been busy." He approved.

"More than a little." She slid her hands into the back pockets of her jeans and canted her head to the side. "I drove up from Dallas because I have to go to Boston, and I thought a road trip together would be fun. Captain Thomas said you'd be free to take the trip, he wasn't sure about times though. Anyway," she rushed on, "even if you have to deploy in a few days, you might like to see the fall colors. They're supposed to be amazing in New England. You can see my show, meet Liam, and we can have some time to ourselves."

"Sweetheart, it sounds wonderful, and we can take all the time you need. I'm not deploying again."

"You're not?" Her eyes rounded. "They discharged you?"

"Honorably," he grinned. "And by my request. There's still a chance I can be recalled, but—"

Shannon squealed and threw her arms around him again. Soaking up the tight squeeze of her embrace, he sighed. "It was time, and I was ready. I might be unemployed for a while though. So, you may be stuck with me hanging around a lot."

Not that Luke wouldn't hire him for something, and Mitch had mentioned a letter from Archer Morgan about his security firm in Dallas, but those were all decisions for later.

"I was so ready to move to a base or hold tight in Dallas, wherever you needed me," she confessed, and his love for her fisted his heart.

"I need you with me, you make me a happy man." After a moment, he added, "And in front of a minister or at a courthouse. You need to be Mrs. Essex as soon as possible."

"Anytime," she said, delight echoing in her tone. "I don't even need some big, fancy wedding. So, we can check into it in Boston."

"Well then, let's get on the road." He grabbed his bag and glanced at the dog. "Does he need a walk?"

"I've been here for three hours. We already went for a lot of walks." Shannon grinned. "I was really early because I couldn't wait to see you. Do you want to drive?"

"New car?" He accepted the keys and opened the Dodge Charger's passenger door. Raphael hopped in and climbed into the backseat to settle on the dog bed waiting for him.

"It's a lease. I didn't know what kind you liked or what I

wanted, so I thought this would be fun and we could decide together."

Together. Damn if the word—and the feeling didn't sound good. He dropped his bag into the trunk with her suitcase then circled the car to slide into the driver's seat. It still had that new car smell. "I like it."

"It's kickass on the highway." She'd buckled her seatbelt but angled so she could stare at him. "I have so much to tell you."

The engine rumbled to life, and Brody put it in gear. "Yeah?"

"Weston pleaded guilty. They haven't sentenced him yet, but everyone says he'll be in prison for years. I've taken some classes at Mike's Place. There's a support group for spouses and families of veterans. James and Lauren recommended it, and I've gone every week. I wanted to know everything you might need me to know." The words spilled out of her like water burbling from a cheerful fountain. "I've also been getting some counseling of my own. James recommended a really great therapist, and she and I are working on my PTSD. And...." she exhaled noisily, her expression tightening. "I sold *Her Marine*."

Surprise filtered through him; she loved the piece. "All of that is fantastic. I'm really proud of you."

"Thank you. You're not mad I sold it?"

"No, not mad. A little surprised though." He reached over and caught her hand.

"In all the craziness, I didn't have a chance to tell you someone bid on it pretty regularly. They topped out at a million dollars."

"Holy shit." Brody blinked. He thought her work was phenomenal, but.... "That's a lot of money."

"I couldn't believe they were serious, so Henry and Jeanine set up a meeting. Turns out, the buyer—Ian Calder—is a Marine, retired. He's also a multi-billionaire or something. They're building a museum in Denver, and they plan to have an entire wing devoted to military service and the Marines in particular. *Her Marine* will be a central part of the exhibit, and eventually, it will travel. When he told me what they were trying to do and how much he would offer, I only agreed if he'd split the check. Half of it will go to Mike's Place and the other half to me."

Sounded almost too good to be true. "Are you sure you trust the guy?"

"Mostly, and Luke checked him out. So did Logan, Archer, Rebel, and Derek. They all gave me calls after they checked into it, and Henry and Jeanine think he's good to go. He even made a donation to Mike's Place to prove his good intentions. But he's part of why we're going to Boston."

"Calder is going to be there?"

"Yeah." She bit her lip. "I won't sell to him if you don't like him."

"Babe, you can do what you want with your work. I just know how much the piece meant to you." She'd been so proud of it, her successful breakthrough.

"I love *Her Marine*, I always will." She brought his hand up to her lips and kissed it. "But I don't need to hold onto it anymore. Not when I have you."

Damn, if it were possible to love her more, he did. "You have me...no getting rid of me now."

The sound of her soft laughter filled the car. "Forever."

"I like the sound of that," he said, content for the first time in years. He didn't know what he would do or where they would go, but all that mattered was he had Shannon. She was safe. She was happy. She was his home.

Mission most definitely accomplished.

~ABOUT THE AUTHOR~

National bestselling author, Heather Long, likes long walks in the park, science fiction, superheroes, Marines, and men who aren't douche bags. Her books are filled with heroes and heroines tangled in romance as hot as Texas summertime. From paranormal historical westerns to contemporary military romance, Heather might switch genres, but one thing is true in all of her stories—her characters drive the books. When she's not wrangling her menagerie of animals, she devotes her time to family and friends she considers family. She believes if you like your heroes so real you could lick the grit off their chest, and your heroines so likable, you're sure you've been friends with women just like them, you'll enjoy her worlds as much as she does.

You can visit Heather at:
www.heatherlong.net

The Always a Marine Series

Always a Marine
Series so Far (in order by release)

Once Her Man, Always Her Man
Luke & Rebecca

Retreat Hell! She Just Got Here
Logan, Jazz & Zach

Tell It to the Marine
James & Lauren
Introduction of Matt McCall and Damon Sinclair
Features an appearance of Logan Cavanaugh

Proud to Serve Her
Damon & Helena
Matt, James, Lauren, Luke and Rebecca mentioned

Her Marine
Brody & Shannon

No Regrets, No Surrender
Logan, Jazz & Zach
James featured

The Marine Cowboy
A.J. & Sheri
Phone call from Luke

The Two and the Proud
Rowdy & Kim

A Marine and a Gentleman
Brenden & Liam
Appearances of James, Logan, Jazz, Shannon, Rebecca, Lauren

Combat Barbie
Kyle & Mary
Jazz makes an appearance via phone

Whiskey Tango Foxtrot
Joe & Melody
James makes an appearance

What Part of Marine Don't You Understand?
Matt & Naomi
Appearances by James and Logan, Damon is mentioned

A Marine Affair
Eli & Rick

Marine Ever After
Paul & Lillianna
Multiple appearances at Luke & Rebecca's wedding

Marine in the Wind
Greg & Georgia
Appearances by A.J. & Sheri

Marine with Benefits
Derek & Kara
Appearance by Logan

A Marine of Plenty
Charlie & Jana
Appearance by Naomi

A Candle for a Marine
Isaac & Zehava
Appearances by Zach & Shannon

Marine Under the Mistletoe
Kaiden & Rowan

Have Yourself a Marine Christmas
Rebel & Noel
Appearances by Derek, Kara, Luke and James

Lest Old Marines Be Forgot
Tom & Brenda
Appearances by Luke, James, Logan, and Damon